MW00809260

Copyright © 2022 by Caitlin Marceau
Cover Art © 2022 by TruBorn Design
Edited by Georgia Papoulias
Published in 2022 by DarkLit Press

ISBN 978-1-7387054-9-8 (Paperback)
ISBN 978-1-998851-00-3 (Ebook)

Tabula Rasa previously published in Phantasmagoria Magazine
Gastric previously published in Blood & Bone by Ghost Orchid Press
Sticky Sweet previously published in Monstroddities by Sliced Up Press
Loop previously published in The Crypt by Ghost Orchid Press
The Amphitrite previously published in Phantasmagoria Magazine
Everything She's Looking For previously published in Dark Hearts by Ghost Orchid Press

.

PRAISE FOR FEMINA

"Gripping, heartbreaking and horrifying by turns, this multifaceted collection perfectly showcases Caitlin Marceau's contemporary style and fresh perspectives. This is horror for the modern age!"
— Antonia Rachel Ward, Author of *Marionette*

"Like a modern Persephone, Caitlin Marceau drags us into the depths to reveal a surprising beauty. These stories feature women struggling to find their place and their voice, their love and their freedom. Whether disaffected, delusional, or demoralized, one can't help but cheer them along, even when they fail. It's exciting to find a fierce, femme voice in Horror and Speculative Fiction."
— C. E. Hoffman, Author of *Sluts and Whores*

"A triumphant call to all the unashamedly monstrous women; especially those who need a reminder that there is no contempt in embracing their brutality."
— Cat Benstead, Managing Editor of Hear Us Scream

"Caitlin takes our deepest insecurities and lays them bare. A MasterClass in gutwrenching horror."
— Rae Knowles Author of *The Stradivarius*

"Marceau has dreamt up a new vocabulary for lives of quiet desperation and fear with this collection of timely stories that will leave you ruined yet desperate for more."
—April Yates, Author of *Ashthorn*

BOOKS BY
CAITLIN MARCEAU

This Is Where We Talk Things Out

Laughlin Hills Community Magazine

Palimpsest

Magnum Opus

A Blackness Absolute

FEMINA

A COLLECTION OF DARK FICTION

CAITLIN MARCEAU

DARKLIT

PRESS

CONTENT WARNING

The story that follows may contain graphic violence and gore.

Please go to the very back of the book for more detailed content warnings.

Beware of spoilers.

To all the women who've shown me what
true strength, compassion, and love looks like

Thank you
xoxoxo

CONTENTS

TABULA RASA

It isn't the pain that wakes her, it's the cold. Tendrils of frost move up her body like climbing ivy. Had this been any other ship, the chill running up her spine might have gone unnoticed, but the Helios isn't known for its cool climate or comfortable working conditions.

On the Helios, everything burns.

The cold dances across her chest and up her neck, finally stopping at her temple. She tries to open her eyes, but they feel heavy, like steel doors frozen shut in the winter. She tries to say something, to scream something, but everything from words to guttural noise gets stuck in the back of her throat. Then, suddenly, the cold is gone.

Cassie exhales through her nose, unable to open her mouth, and listens to the emptiness around her. Someone is in the room with her, but she's not sure who it is. She tunes out the noise of the blood pumping through her veins and her shaky breathing, and listens to the silence around her.

The last thing she remembers is… she's not sure. The thoughts swirl away like fog at her fingertips. She remembers being in a dark hallway and hearing noise somewhere behind her. She remembers trying to find the source of the noise and then… nothing. Emptiness. The memory fades away. When she reaches for it again, it slips through her fingers in pools of smoke.

There's movement to her left and she strains to hear the—

Pain.

It crashes into her like an icy wave that cuts down to her bones and she panics that she's drowning. But she's not drowning, not yet. She can still draw air in and she tries to focus on this. The pain is overwhelming and her muscles clench and spasm, jaw aching as her teeth crunch against each other. Her eyes roll back in her head and she can feel tears building up under her eyelids.

As the cold swallows her whole, she tries to breathe.

She's not sure how long she's been out, but the cold is back and creeping along her flesh. It's what pulls her out of the darkness and roots her back in her body. She feels helpless, something she's never been before, and the realization makes her furious. She fights against the cold and the heaviness in her limbs. She grits her teeth and pulls against the invisible restraints on her body. Something in the air around her loosens, and a howl rips through her as she forces her eyes open and sits up on the table. She blinks a few times as her eyes adjust to the darkness around her.

It's the empty mess hall of the Helios, and she exhales with relief. For a moment, she'd worried she'd been stolen from the ship.

Of all the rooms aboard the vessel, she loves this one the most. Although it seems small and sterile at a first glance, with metal tables and chairs filling the space, its farthest wall made of floor-to-ceiling glass is what makes the room something exceptional. Aside from the brig, it's the only place aboard the Helios that doesn't need to be kept as stiflingly hot or blindingly dark. For this reason, the mess hall is the only place the crewmates (when there were crewmates) could come to escape the oppressiveness of the ship. Looking out into space makes her feel small but somehow bigger than herself. She can peer out into the universe and know that, while she is alone, she is part of everything.

She watches the swirling lights and nebulous vortexes as she opens and closes her stiff hands before massaging feeling back into her legs. As she begins working the taut muscles in her shoulders, she realizes she's not alone. The thing stands in the corner of the room, staring out at the universe too.

Cassie practically stops breathing, waiting for it to do something.

"How are you awake?" it finally asks.

She doesn't answer.

After a long moment of silence, the thing turns back and looks at her. It's naked and has been crying; the tear tracks running from its brown eyes and over freckled cheeks glimmer in the starlight. Its flowing red hair looks like fire in the dark and beads of sweat gather on its chest and roll down its temple. As if ashamed of its nakedness, it covers itself with its hands and looks away from Cassie's gaze.

It looks just like me.

The thought should horrify her, but it doesn't, and this fact is what causes her discomfort.

"I miss Sam," it says, blinking away tears. "I miss him so much. How do you bear it?"

"Who's Sam?" Cassie asks.

"And Lucas," it answers. "His absence, it's like—"

"How do you know Lucas?"

"He was our husband."

Cassie's heart beats faster and her body trembles as she shakes her head violently from side to side. "Bullshit. He's *my* husband. You keep his name out of your mouth. You don't know him! You don't know anything about hi—"

"But we do know about him. Not everything, not yet. We didn't get to those memories. We haven't absorbed them yet. It's always hard to start with the end and work backwards. Lucas is no exception."

"What do you—"

"We know that it was human error in automation that caused it. We know he was too far from the other ships to get help in time. We know we spoke to him in those final moments."

Her hands are clammy and her throat is tight as she listens to the double talk about Lucas. "I don't know what you're talking about—"

"I know why we hold on to Sam so tightly," the creature says, clutching its chest in pain.

"I don't know anyone named Sam."

"You did. You don't anymore. Only I know him now. Only I can remember him anymore. I'm so sorry to have stolen that from you."

"What are you?" Cassie looks around the room, mentally calculating the distance between her table and the door, trying to judge whether the thing would stop her from escaping or if she could get away.

"I'm you, or I am now. I used to be someone else before today, and when this form gives out at the end of its life cycle, I suppose I'll be someone else when that tomorrow comes," it says, looking down at its imitation body.

"You're not me," Cassie spits.

"Aren't I? I look like you, I think like you, I *feel* like you. I know this tremendous loss like you."

"I don't know what you're talking about."

"I know, but you did. Now it's only mine."

"You still haven't answered my question. I asked you what the fuck you are."

"I don't know what I am anymore," it admits. "My kind exists to learn, to experience as many forms of life as we can to understand what makes you *you*. We absorb, we become, and we move on. To fulfill our purpose is our greatest joy and our greatest sorrow, because we know it means sacrificing innocent life. And yet, to immortalize each life and record them in our shared memory is an honour. Your life will become a legacy. You will never be forgotten. Please, do not think of this as an end, but as a beginning. You and your love for Sam, your love for Lucas, will live forever."

The double moves closer, smiling gently.

Cassie backs up, moving towards the mess door.

"Please don't go," it says, looking sadly at Cassie and the door. "We only want to—"

Cassie doesn't give it a chance to finish. She turns on her heel and runs.

After spending over 26,000 hours aboard the Helios, Cassie can navigate the hallways in complete darkness. Her feet echo in the empty halls and sweat gathers on her skin, the air now burning hot in contrast to the bracing cold from earlier. She hopes she's making enough noise for the creature to find her; she needs to lead it away from where she has to go. She runs as fast as her legs will take her, letting her body take charge and guide her through the dark to the brig. She rounds the corner and runs to the end of the hall before stopping abruptly. Quietly, she moves back the way she came and ducks under a pipe, the heat burning her skin as she crawls quietly behind it. The air is scorching here, as boiling water surges through the metal tube, and her skin blisters as she waits.

It doesn't take long for her double to run past, feet clumsy in the dark. It may have stolen some of Cassie's memories of the Helios, but those would be shrouded in darkness. The Helios is a transport vessel that moves specialized raw materials, along with the occasional skilled labourer, to colonies around the galaxy. The materials need to be kept hot and away from sunlight, and so the ship is like a blackened furnace floating through space. Cassie doesn't rely on her mind to move through the ship, she relies on muscle memory.

Something her duplicate's body cannot remember.

Once its footsteps have faded down the hall, Cassie creeps out from behind the pipe, her skin raw and blistered, and makes her way back to her sleeping quarters and the communication transmitter inside. Although it can't call the command centre like the one located in the brig, it's mobile and on a secure line. At least she can call home and then Lucas can—

Why aren't I home?

The thought stops her in her tracks. Dizzy, Cassie leans

against the walls and tries to catch her breath. She closes her eyes and thinks as far back as she can, trying to remember how she got on the ship. How she got on *Lucas'* ship.

She thinks back to her husband and how he'd always hated his job, but because the pay was good and he loved his crewmates he kept coming back. How he'd always loved the camaraderie of working on the Helios, at least until the automation had slowly replaced his friends. She thinks about how the Helios would take him away from home for years at a time and how she begged him not to go on his last voyage, which had taken him away from Cassie shortly after their third anniversary. She remembers talking to him at night when he'd call her on the communicator, how he'd sit in the empty mess hall with the glory of space behind him and tell her how much he loved her. She remembers him calling her, that something had failed in the programming of the Helios on its journey home and that—

Nothing. The rest is smoke.

There's noise in the hallway. Her heart threatens to jump out of her chest and her throat closes in panic as she listens to the creature move clumsily in the darkness. It stumbles into pipes and bumps into walls, blind in the dark. Once the noise of it searching for her fades away, Cassie forces herself to move once again. She wants to run as fast as her body will allow, but she creeps carefully through the maze that is the Helios. She doesn't want her double to know where she's going, at least not this time.

When she gets to her room, she makes sure she's alone before quickly opening the door and closing it gently behind her. Her room is one of the few spaces on the ship that's allowed to have light, and she doesn't want a sudden stream of it in the darkness to alert her duplicate to her whereabouts.

The room can barely be considered a room. Inside is enough space to fit a bed, a nightstand, and a chest filled with clothes. On the nightstand is a small electric lantern that fills the room with yellow light. Beside it rests a framed photo of Cassie and Lucas on one of their first dates.

It hadn't been love at first sight for the two of them. He'd existed quietly in her life for years before she ever really noticed him. They'd gone to school together as children and then shared a few classes as adults. It was only when they bumped into each other a few years after graduation at a farmer's market that he'd found the courage to ask her out, and she'd surprised them both by saying yes. They'd dated for less than six months before he'd asked her to marry him and she'd accepted, and before a full year had passed they were wed.

The transmitter lies on top of a piece of folded paper in the centre of her bed. She lets the weight of her body fall onto the mattress as she picks up the device and turns it on, the small screen glowing to life. She double-checks that the knob is turned to the right frequency, and her muscles take over to dial a number she doesn't recognize.

"Mommy!" a young boy shouts at her, filling the small space with noise.

"Where's Lucas?" Cassie asks.

"Mommy, Nana took me to see the—"

"Where is Lucas?" she shouts, her chest swelling with panic at the sight of the child and the sudden sound of footsteps approaching from down the hall.

"Who?" he asks. "Mommy, you won't believe how-"

Cassie turns the communicator off and clips it to her belt. She stands up fast, wind knocking the folded sheet of paper off the bed and onto the ground. She picks it up, stuffs it in her pocket without thinking, and leaves her room, running for the ship's core. She might not be able to save herself, but with a bit of luck, she might be able to shut down the Helios and stop the creature from ever getting off of the vessel.

The closer she gets to the core, the hotter the air around her gets. Her skin feels raw and swollen, and her lips crack from the heat and dehydration. She doesn't know anything about the mechanics that propel the vessel through space, but she hopes that if she pulls out enough wiring and jams enough components, the ship will be out of commission long enough for the air to cut off or to veer far enough off course that it's lost to space forever. She opens the door to the engine room—the hot metal blisters her skin—and closes it behind her, locking it from the inside.

The communicator on her hip begins to ring. She double checks that the door is securely locked before she answers.

"Hello?"

"Cassie, hey!" her mother says through the screen, frowning. "Sam says that you called but then hung up on h-"

"Who the hell is Sam? And why are you answering this line? Where's Lucas?"

Her mother is quiet for an uncomfortably long time before she answers. "Sweetie, you're scaring me."

"Mom, where the fuck is Lucas?"

"But you know what happened."

"Mom, I need you to just tell me."

"Why? You've been working so hard to put this behind you."

"Please, Mom, just—"

"Cassie, what's going on? I'm worried about you. You don't seem right and I'm—"

"Mom! Just tell me where Lucas is!"

"Pine Ridge Memorial," her mother finally says.

"What?"

"We buried him at Pine Ridge Memorial almost five years ago, Cassie."

"What?" Cassie chokes.

"Sweetie, please, just tell me what's going on."

Her legs go weak; it feels like her whole body is being dragged under water, and she struggles to breathe. Her mother says something over the transmitter, but she doesn't hear it. She doesn't hear anything aside from the dull pounding of her heartbeat in her ears. Her mother yells something at her, but it's gibberish. It doesn't make sense to Cassie. Nothing does. She turns off the communicator and drops it onto the floor.

"I'm so sorry," her double says through the barred window slit in the steel door. "I had hoped to spare us this pain, this knowing. But now it is too late."

Cassie breathes in through her nose and out through her mouth, trying to clear her mind. She tries to think back to Lucas, to his death, but the memories are gone and all that's left is emptiness and mist.

The communicator rings on the ground beside her, but she ignores it. When it rings a second time, she turns the device off and forces herself to her feet. She looks around the small room, the walls lined with square panels and pipes, and settles on a wall that looks promising. She begins pulling open the nearby covers, exposing the cables and electronics inside.

"Please, don't!" the creature says, desperately, banging on the door. "Please! If you do this, Sam will be alone! He needs his mother. He *deserves* his mother," it sobs.

"I don't know who the fuck Sam is!" Cassie screams.

"He's our son!" the creature says through the metal. "He's our son, and we love him more than anything. We keep a picture of him in our room and we hold it close when we're lonely. We call him every night on the communicator. He's the reason we're on this ship. He's the reason our lives have meaning. I love him."

Cassie stops, the crumpled paper in her pocket heavy as a rock. She takes it out of her pocket and looks at it closely. It's hard to see in the dim light of the Helios' core, so she turns on the communicator's screen and shines it over the image. The newborn in the photo looks at her with big round eyes, the same shocking blue that Lucas' were. He's too young to have much hair, but what little he does have poking out from beneath his striped hospital cap is red like her own. The baby is fat and happy, his chubby cheeks framing plump lips. He's looking out at whoever is taking the photo from the comfort of his mother's arms. From *her* arms.

"If you could remember him, you would know how much you love him too," the creature tells her.

"But I can't. I don't."

"Then think of Lucas." Cassie stops moving, her chest constricting in pain at the thought of him. "Sam is Lucas' son too."

"Lucas is dead! He died on this fucking ship! You heard what she said."

"We know he did. But think about it, why are we here?"

"What?"

"Why are we on the Helios?"

"I…" Cassie stops to think, but her memories feel thick like fog and disappear when she reaches out for them. "I don't know."

"To pay our debt."

"What debt?"

"The one we took to have Sam. We signed the contract that put us here for these last three years. We promised we'd serve on this ship, alone, in exchange for the procedure that would impregnate us with Lucas' child posthumously. All we had to do was answer their call. How could we say no?"

Cassie's heart beats fast in panic and her eyes sting as she tries to remember how she came to be on the ship, but she can't. She thinks of all the times she's called home over the years and strains to remember who she's been speaking to. She pictures her mother's face, happy but lined with concern, and then… nothing. It's just more swirling fog that escapes her faster the more she tries.

"I don't remember him."

"But we would do anything for him. I know we would! We would do anything for Lucas' child. For *our* child."

"Then give him back to me. If you love him like I love him, give him back to me."

"I can't," it cries. "I wish I could, but I can't. Once we take, we cannot give back. I'm so sorry, but *please* don't punish him by taking away his mother."

"I'm his mother," Cassie says, the words feeling wrong in her mouth.

She'd always wanted to be a mother, even before she knew what that really meant. She'd babied dolls and looked after the younger kids in school. While she'd never believed in destiny, she'd always joked hers had been motherhood.

For the label to now taste so bitter on her tongue breaks her heart.

"You are. Please, if you promise you won't leave him, then I'll go and let this version of us be lost to time."

Cassie stays quiet for a long time, her duplicate waiting on the other side of the door. Eventually, she puts the photo back in her pocket, returns the panels to the wall, and unlocks the door.

"You would do that? You would leave?"

"We would die for him. We love our boy more than anything in the world. He needs us," the creature says. "He needs his mother."

Cassie looks at the creature, seeing the worry and anguish that lines its face. That lines *her* face.

"But that isn't me."

The double tilts her head, confused. "Of course it is."

The original shakes hers. "It's not anymore. I don't know this child. I don't love this child. I *want* to, and maybe in time I would have, but I don't. All I feel is grief. I can't be his mother. "

"He needs us," she says.

"He needs *you*. He needs his mother."

She stares at her, confused, before realization sets in. Her smile is lined with sadness and she nods, understanding.

"Will it hurt?" the original asks.

"Yes, but mostly you'll just feel—"

"Cold."

The new Cassie chuckles sadly. "Yes. You'll feel cold, and then you won't feel anything at all."

She lies on the table of the mess hall, taking in the view from the window one last time before closing her eyes. The cold finds her skin in the warmth of the Helios and begins to spread throughout her body. At first, it feels like cold arms wrapping around her, but soon she shivers as though she's been submerged in cold water. And then the pain hits.

It's the worst pain she's ever experienced.

She grabs the sides of the metal table, fingers digging into the hard surface as her muscles clench. Her body guides her through the process, knowing what it's doing even if she doesn't. It pushes and shakes from the effort, muscles straining as she screams for strength and release. She feels like she's tearing in two and she cries from the enormity of it all.

Her body knows this pain. It's been here before, even if her mind doesn't remember. The realization of this startles her. She opens her eyes, tears spilling over and onto her cheeks.

She holds him close, breathing in the smell of baby shampoo and freshly cut grass one last time. She holds his little body tight against her own, surprised at how big he's gotten in his first year.

She doesn't cry, even though she wants to. The last thing she wants is for this memory to be a sad one. It's the last time she'll see him like this for a long time. When she eventually gets back, he'll be almost five.

The thought crushes her.

She forces herself to smile through the pain and kisses him on his cheeks, on his button nose, and his forehead.

"I love you so much," she whispers to Sam. "More than you'll ever know."

She screams one last time as regret floods her body. Sam's face turns to smoke and is gone. She sobs silently, unsure of why she's upset, as parts of her fade away. The faces in her memory dissolve into mist as her life unwinds. Soon, there's nothing left to keep her tethered, and she fades into nothingness.

She looks out the giant window of the Helios' mess hall. It's quiet once again on the ship, and she's eager to come home. In a few days, she'll be landing. In a few days, she'll hold her son. But, for now, the communicator will have to do. She flips on the device, turns to the right frequency, and dials the number.

"Mommy!" Sam cries on the other end of the transmitter. "Nana, look, it's Mommy!"

Cassie smiles.

GASTRIC

The room smells like rubbing alcohol and floor cleaner, and although it's warm, Billie is cold in her thin hospital gown. She shivers on the gurney, partly because of the thin fabric that opens in the back, partly because of nerves. Her husband sits on the worn-in armchair next to the bed and scrolls through his Instagram feed, stopping every few minutes to like a photo. She pretends not to notice when he double taps an image of a twenty-something woman in a bikini.

"What time is it?" she asks, fidgeting with the plastic identification bracelet fastened around her wrist. There are no clocks on the walls, which only heightens her suspicion that time isn't passing at all within the confines of her room. Alfie swipes his finger across his phone and frowns.

"It's just after two. The doctor's late."

"Maybe this is a sign," she says, immediately regretting her decision to speak up about the issue.

Alfie sighs, leaning to one side so he can slip his phone into his pocket, before locking eyes with her. "Are we really having this conversation again?"

"No, I'm not trying to… well, yeah, actually," she finally admits, looking away from him. "I'm nervous and, honestly, I still really don't know if I want to do this. It just… I don't know, it seems extreme."

"Billie, how many times have you tried to lose weight on your own?"

"I don't know."

"Neither do I, but I know it's been a lot. And I know this because I've had to live with you through each weird diet phase you've gone through. There were shakes, bars, something involving wheatgrass and a juicer, fasting, group meetings, premade meals—"

"I know, I know. But diet culture is fucked and science shows that diets don't work and—"

"They don't work for *you*." The words are like a slap in the face and she feels winded. "But that's okay," he continues in a softer voice, "having that level of willpower is tough and just isn't for everyone. And even having the willpower to lose the weight without help doesn't mean you'll have the willpower to keep it off. It just doesn't seem like something you'd be able to do. But the procedure you're going to have? It'll be *super* manageable for you afterwards. That way, you won't have the fear of getting, uh, you know, *fat* again looming over you for the rest of your life."

She looks down at herself and runs a hand over her stomach, gently feeling her body through the threadbare gown. It's soft and Rubenesque and—despite what her husband thinks—beautiful. She'd always been bigger than the other girls growing up, a fact that had never bothered her until her grandma had said something about it in front of her family over turkey dinner one Christmas. It had been the start of a life-long battle with weight, self-love, and her ability to navigate the world comfortably. She'd continued to gain weight through most of high school, but lost a fair amount after puberty hit her like a brick a year before graduation. It had been this leaner body that she'd started college with, and the one Alfie had fallen in love with nearly ten years ago.

She'd started gaining weight before their wedding when the stress of planning the event had started to feel like too much. It hadn't been enough weight gain to bother her, but Alfie had started to notice and comment on the change. He started acting cold towards her, less physically affectionate, and it wasn't long after that that his eyes began wandering when they were out in public. She didn't want to call it quits with him—she *loved* him—so she decided the only reasonable thing to do was wage war on her body. Unfortunately, it was an uphill battle that had left her heavier than when she'd started. While she wasn't angry about the change in her body, it was getting harder to ignore the judgmental comments and sideways glances her husband had been giving her. When he brought up the procedure, she felt like the only way to save her marriage was to agree to it.

But sitting on the uncomfortable bed in the sterile room, Billie was regretting her decision.

"You keep saying 'fat' like it's a bad word. It's not. And it hurts when you talk like this," she admits.

Alfie rolls his eyes in annoyance and crosses his arms over his chest. "I'm sorry if I hurt your feelings, but let's be honest about this. This operation is your best shot at a *normal* life," he stresses the word. "Don't you want that? Don't you want to be able to shop at any store you want? Don't you want to be able to run after our kids, you know, when we have them?"

She opens her mouth to argue her point, but Dr. Fortin chooses this moment to show up. He's a tall man with a receding hairline. He's dressed in navy scrubs and a white lab coat, and he carries a silver clipboard that comically dwarfs the papers resting atop it. He pulls a pen out from his breast pocket and clicks the end of it before scribbling something at the top of a page.

"Today's the big day!" he says with a smile, looking up from the sheet of paper. "How are you feeling?"

"Excited," Alfie answers for her. "We're both very excited."

"Good! I'm glad to hear! So I'm just going to—"

"Actually," Billie interrupts, "I'm pretty nervous about everything. And I know this is last minute, but I'm just... I'm having second thoughts about everything, you know?" she admits, despite her husband's audible annoyance.

"That's perfectly normal," the doctor says, crossing the room and taking a seat at the end of her gurney. "What's on your mind?"

"I'm worried I'm making a mistake with this. That I'm having something so invasive done to lose a few pounds and that—"

"It's invasive, yes, but minimally so! Remember,

everything is being done laparoscopically, so while you'll have a few scars afterwards, each will be quite small—the biggest one will be where we insert the device and it won't even be two inches—and they should mostly fade away over time. As for your comment about it being a few pounds, remember that we're hoping this operation will get you down by almost a hundred pounds and that weight loss is nearly impossible for people with your BMI. And while this procedure isn't a quick fix, it's a tool that can help you drop the excess weight."

"Yeah, I guess."

"If it's any reassurance, I know that if my daughters were fat they'd be happier thin and I'd have them do this same surgery in a heartbeat," he says happily. "Besides, just think of how good it'll feel to be pretty, right?"

"That's what I keep telling her," Alfie adds.

The comments sting and upset her. She hates their conflation of beauty and weight, and how they've weaponized her size to cut at her sense of self-worth. Her face turns crimson and shame sets in, embarrassed at her husband's quick agreement with the doctor. *Am I not already pretty?* she asks him with her eyes. *Do you find me repulsive?*

Looking at the hospital band on her wrist and the unfriendly room, she already knows the answer.

"So," the doctor continues, not giving Billie a chance to speak, "I'm just going to go over what we're going to be doing today, answer any last-minute questions you might have, and then you'll be directed to the first floor for some pre-op blood work. Sounds good?"

"Yes."

"Excellent! So, today we're going to be inserting the Gastra-Sphaera GR into your stomach laparoscopically. Pre-insertion, the device is a little smaller than a loonie, but once we inflate it with the slow-release hormone solution it'll have a diameter of roughly two and a half—maybe three—inches. It'll be fixed to the wall of your stomach, so there's no risk of you accidentally passing it."

"Okay. Will I feel it? Like, after the operation, when I

wake up, will I feel it inside?"

"You might initially. Some patients say it feels like a small weight has been placed in their stomachs, others don't notice it at all. Less than 0.03% of patients report feeling the device after the three-month adjustment period. So if you do feel it, it'll only be a temporary discomfort, especially since the solution in the device is released gradually over the next eighteen months."

"Okay."

"You'll be placed under general anesthesia for the procedure and kept under observation overnight, just to be safe. Assuming all goes well, you'll be back home this time tomorrow. Now, I just want to reiterate that this isn't a cure for obesity." Billie shifts uncomfortably at the use of the harsh clinical term. "It's a tool to get it under control. Because of the weight and size of the Gastra-Sphaera GR, you're going to feel full faster, and thanks to the slow-release hormone to help control your body's production of Ghrelin, you're not going to be hungry or have many food cravings. This will give you roughly eighteen months to re-learn nutrition, how to eat a balanced diet, and how to practice better portion control. If you stick to the plan we've given you and put in the work, you'll be able to successfully lose the hundred pounds and keep it off. Exciting, right?"

"Very," Alfie answers.

Billie just nods her head.

"Did you have any questions for me before I get going?" Dr. Fortin asks happily.

She does, she has dozens of them, but she shakes her head and smiles.

"Great! Let's get you downstairs for the blood work and get this show on the road!"

With that, he leads her out of the room and down the hall. Alfie watches her go before turning his attention back to his phone.

"Your name?" the receptionist asks.

"Billie Ouellet."

"And you have an appointment today?"

"Yes, with Dr. Fortin. It's for the two-week follow-up and to have the sutures removed."

"I'll need your Medicare."

Billie opens her wallet and takes out the card, passing it to the woman. The receptionist looks at the card before she places it in the designated groove of the old-fashioned manual card imprinter, places a sheet of prescription paper on top, and slides the handle of the machine. She does this two more times—one on a second sheet of prescription paper and the other on a hospital form—before handing back the card and motioning to the nearby waiting area.

Billie takes a seat, shoving the card back into her wallet, and looks around the familiar space. The walls are eggshell white and decorated with abstract art in sky blue and grass green, each illuminated by a small light fixed to its wooden frame. The floor is linoleum made to look like white ceramic tiles, and the chairs match the picture frames. The vinyl cushions are thin and uncomfortable and do little to soften the hard seat beneath her. She drums her fingers on the armrest as she waits for her turn.

"Billie Ouellet?" a nurse calls out.

She stands, collecting her purse from its spot on the ground next to the chair leg, and follows the nurse into the doctor's office where she's weighed on a digital scale before being instructed to sit on the examination table. It's another ten-minute wait before Dr. Fortin walks in, all smiles and good spirits, and he takes a seat on a swivel chair across from Billie.

"Well, look at you!" he says cheerfully. "How have you been?"

"Umm, good, I guess?"

"Good? Not amazing? Your weigh-in shows you've

already dropped 16 pounds. That's phenomenal!"

"Yeah, sort of."

He frowns and leans back in his chair. "So, tell me, what's got you down about your success so far? If it's that you haven't lost enough, remember that this is a process, and you need to trust in it for your long-term success."

"No, I know. It actually feels a bit fast. But, umm, I think something's wrong," she admits.

"What do you mean?"

"Well, it's been two weeks since the operation and I'm still not able to keep anything down. Like, I can get water in and take the occasional sip of a protein shake, but I can't keep a full shake down yet."

"That's normal," he says, waving the air dismissively with one hand. "Your body is still adjusting to the Gastra-Sphaera GR. It's normal that you're feeling too full to eat much."

"But that's the thing, I'm *not* full," she says in frustration. "I'm *never* full. And when I try to ingest anything, it comes back up."

"Well, you should only be drinking things right now. You're still on the liquid diet phase of this procedure. If you're trying to eat things earlier than you're supposed to—"

"I'm not! If I drink anything, whether it's clear broth or a protein shake, I can only keep a few teaspoons down. But, even then, most of it just makes me throw up."

He nods his head before jotting something down on a paper in her file. "Anything else?"

"Well, yeah, actually. I can feel it."

"Feel what?"

"The device. I know you said some people would be able to after the surgery, but it's like this hot ball of metal in my gut. I just, I don't know. It doesn't feel right."

The doctor nods his head, jots something else down on the paper, before closing her file on the desk. He leans back in his chair, smiling, and crosses one arm over the other across his chest. "This is your first surgery, correct?" She nods. "It's normal for people in your position to get anxious after having a procedure done. The weight of the Gastra-Sphaera GR in your stomach is perfectly normal. It's only uncomfortable because it's not familiar to your body, but it will be. You just need to give it time."

"But—"

"The same goes for your hunger and not being able to keep food down. The hormone in the device uses a slow-release, and your body hasn't gotten used to it, which means you might still be hungry for another week or two until your body has had enough time to adjust to the hormone. When it comes to keeping your food down, you just had an operation done! Your stomach's going to be inflamed and sensitive where the incisions were made, and this inflammation and discomfort will be temporarily exacerbated by the weight affixed to the wall of your stomach. This is all perfectly normal."

She places a protective hand over her stomach. Her skin is numb where the cuts were made, nerves severed, and the sensation of her fingers on her chest is dulled. "I know, it's just, I can't explain it. It feels like something isn't right."

He nods patronizingly. "It doesn't feel right because you've never had to deal with this before, which is why you're having such a dramatic response to the healing process. But I promise it's perfectly normal. Just do me a favour and trust the process."

The voice in the back of her mind tells her to push the issue. Instead, Billie just nods.

She smiles from her seat on the bench, watching as the pigeons hop and flap around her, pecking at the scattered crumbs and French fries that have been thrown on the sidewalk by passersby who've ignored the sign reading *Don't Feed The Birds*. They stare at her with their big eyes and bigger bodies, bold enough to take up space in such a busy park, but smart enough to move when an excited child runs at them with open arms. Two birds puff themselves up and dance around abandoned bread crust, making her laugh. The movement jostles her stomach, and she stills from the pain of it.

The Gastra-Sphaera GR feels like a brick in her stomach, threatening to squish her insides every time she moves. She leans back on the bench, stomach gurgling and her mouth watering as she thinks about the food she desperately wants. She wonders if, given enough time, she'll become like the birds: desperate for scraps and celebrating every bite she gets down. Billie sincerely hopes not.

She runs a hand through her hair, blanching when she sees how much of it has come out, tangled around her fingers. She tries to fluff up her bob, hoping that the short style, curls, and extra volumizing hairspray hides some of her baldness. Her heart hurts just thinking about the way her hair used to look, with waves and body for days. Now, it awkwardly frames her too-thin face, revealing bald patches of her pale scalp when the wind blows. She prays that isn't the case today, not when she's seeing her best friend for the first time since the procedure.

"Hey!" a familiar voice calls out from behind her. She smiles, gets to her feet—limbs heavy with the familiar feeling of constant exhaustion—and waves to her friend. "Oh my God! You look so tiny!" Florina shouts with excitement.

"Oh, uh, yeah!" Billie says.

"You're like, what? Half your size already?" Florina asks.

"Umm, no, not yet." *But soon*, Billie thinks with dread.

"You look so good. *So good*. I can't believe I've been sitting on my ass, letting myself go in a shitty office, and you've been living your best life looking hot as fuck."

"I don't know if I'd say that," Billie admits.

She'd been off from work since the surgery. Although the Gastra-Sphaera GR procedure promised a speedy recovery time, with patients being able to return to work in as little as three days, Alfie had convinced her to take a leave of absence from the library for the summer so she could "focus on making sustainable changes." She suspects that what he really meant was "so you can work out and tighten up any extra skin." But since the operation, she's been too exhausted to do much beyond going for light walks or sitting on the balcony. She doesn't have the energy for anything anymore. It's been almost four months since the device was implanted, and she still can't keep food down. Although Billie is now able to keep *most* of her protein shakes down, she has to drink them throughout the day and can't take big sips without becoming nauseated. To make matters even more frustrating, she has to water them down, otherwise the thick powder and milk makes her throw up.

"I would! You look incredible!"

"Oh, well, thanks."

"Don't mention it," Florina says, looking her friend up and down with an impressed smile. "So, are you in the mood for coffee? Lunch? Both? Like, are you hungry?"

Yes, Billie thinks desperately. She's ravenous, and she misses the taste of solid food. Her stomach is weighed down and filled up by Gastra-Sphaera GR, but it does nothing to satiate her desire to eat.

"Maybe just a coffee for me," she says with a forced smile, wanting to cry.

The two of them make their way down the block. Billie asks her friend to walk slowly so that she can enjoy the sights, not wanting to admit that she's tired and badly in need of protein. When they get there, Billie waits impatiently in line as she eyes one of the small tables out on the coffee shop's patio.

"Hey there, what can I getcha?" the young barista asks with a smile.

"Umm," Billie pauses to look at the menu. "Can I have a latte with skim milk and no sugar, please."

"Sure thing. Can I interest you in one of our delicious pastries today?" the barista asks, pointing to the selection in the display window.

"No, thanks."

The barista gives her the total and she taps her card against the machine, waiting for it to beep and confirm her purchase before she waits for her drink at the end of the counter. Florina meets her at the end of the counter holding a croissant on a small white plate as she tucks her receipt into the open mouth of her purse.

"God, you have some willpower. I can never say no to their baked goods. It's why I have an ass the size of Florida."

Billie laughs as she takes her freshly-made drink off the counter, but she can't keep her focus off of the pastry in her friend's hand. Florina says something else, but Billie doesn't hear her and doesn't catch it when her friend repeats herself.

"Hey!" Florina says louder and Billie jumps. "You okay?" she asks, grabbing her drink and following Billie to one of the empty tables.

"Yeah, yeah. Sorry."

"You zoned out *hard* back there. Everything alright?"

Billie stares at the croissant as Florina takes a bite, her stomach rumbling and mouth watering. She swallows her saliva and looks at her friend.

"Honestly? Not really."

"Why? What's up?"

She blows gently on her steaming drink before taking a sip of it. "I think something went wrong with the operation."

"What do you mean?"

"I, uh, I haven't been able to keep food down since they put the thing in me, and I'm hungry all the fucking time. Like, *all* the time. It wakes me up in the middle of the night and makes me want to scream."

"So just eat something."

"I *can't*. I literally can't. That's what I'm saying. Everything, *everything* comes back up. My stomach can't handle it. Like, I tried making myself soup the other night and after a few spoonfuls it was like a scene from the fucking *Exorcist*," she admits, voice hitching in her throat. "I keep staring into my fridge and wanting to eat everything in sight, but know that I'll fucking puke it up. It's bad, and I'm really worried. Alfie doesn't seem to think anything's wrong. He just keeps telling me to wait for my six-month follow-up. But like, he only cares about me being skinny. I wouldn't have even gone through with this stupid fucking thing if it wasn't for him."

She touches her stomach and her muscles clench from hunger, the weight of the Gastra-Sphaera GR a constant reminder of her decision. Everyone promised this operation would give her better health, a better body, a better life. While she'd never believed their fatphobic promises, she had believed Alfie when he said that the surgery would fix their relationship. But like all the other promises that had been made to her, this one was empty too.

"Look," Florina says, gulping down the last of her pastry, "I know this isn't what you want to hear, but I think some of this might all be in your head."

"What?"

"Well, just, my friend's friend had the surgery and *she* was fine. She went through a pretty similar thing where she couldn't keep the food down for a while, but like, it was fine after a few months. I think your body's probably still adjusting to everything and it'll work itself out, but you're so worried about this operation that the stress is making your symptoms seem worse to you than they really are, you know? Like, I don't want to say you're being a hypochondriac, but like, you kind of are."

Billie takes another sip of her drink, feeling more alone than she ever has. "Yeah, uh, maybe you're right."

"I'm definitely right. Like, you look *so* beautiful right now. And, besides," she laughs, "just think of all the clothes you can afford now that you don't need food."

She holds onto the side of the toilet, stomach clenching and throat burning as the food makes its way back up her throat. She hates the acidic and rancid taste of bile and the feeling of half-eaten foods as they creep back up her esophagus. The vomit hits the water but is drowned out by the noise of coughing. When she's finally done, she rinses her mouth with clean water from the bottle next to her on the ground, spits it into the bowl too, and flushes.

Billie leans across the bathroom floor, finding the CorningWare dish with the leftover chicken inside, and puts the red lid back on top of it. She mentally crosses "leftover fajitas" off of her list, before picking the next one to try. She eyes a Tupperware with beef stew and pops the lid off, taking a small bite of potato and carrot. She chews it until it's practically paste and swallows, hoping it will stay down, but it doesn't take long for her body to disappoint her. She runs back to the toilet and heaves, stomach aching.

"What the fuck is this?" Alfie shouts from the doorway. She hadn't mentioned her plans to experiment with solid food when he left for work in the morning. She'd wrongly assumed she'd have found something her body could keep down before he got home.

She doesn't get a chance to turn and answer him as her body forces bile out through her mouth, but she can imagine his surprise. The bathroom is full of leftovers, boxes from the cupboard, and even some frozen foods taken out of the deep freeze. Plastic cutlery lies abandoned on the ground and counters, forgotten the moment Billie's body rebelled against her.

"Sorry," she says, exhausted, spitting the last of it into the water. "I'll clean everything up, I promise."

"What the fuck are you even doing?"

She rests the side of her face against her arm, which is draped over the bowl. It's bony and uncomfortable, but she's too tired to care.

"Trying to keep something, *anything*, down. I'm so

fucking hungry."

"So then you drink a protein shake! You don't binge like this!"

"I'm not bingeing, I'm testing out which foods agree with me. So far none of them do." Her stomach is sore from hours of heaving, but it's the pain of the Gastra-Sphaera GR fixed like a hot ball of lead to the inside of her body that she can't stop focusing on. "I hate this. I'm miserable. I want this fucking thing out."

"Don't be dramatic."

She finally looks up at him with a glare. "What the fuck did you say?"

"I said 'don't be dramatic.' Without the Gastra you'd still be fat. Now, you're thin and gorgeous and you have your life back. You just need to give your body time to adjust to the hormones and trust the process. But apparently," he gestures to the food around the room, "you'd rather throw all your progress away."

"Progress? Is that what you're calling it?" Billie says, voice echoing in the porcelain bowl.

"What else would you ca—"

"I'm fucking starving!" she shouts. "I'm hungry *all the time* and nobody cares! It's been five months since I ate anything solid. I'm *hungry*! I'm in pain *all the time*. My stomach is on fucking fire because of this Gastra. I hate it! And you're telling me I'm dramatic because I'm upset?"

He rolls his eyes. "If you really felt this way, you should have said something about it."

"That's *all* I've been doing!" she screams. "But you're not fucking listening. I hate this fucking implant. I regret getting it done."

I regret listening to you.

She doesn't say it, but the thought hangs heavy in the air between them.

"Then if that's how you really feel," he finally says as he turns on his heel to walk away, "you should tell Dr. Fortin."

She listens to his footsteps as he heads back down the

hall, the floor hard and uncomfortable under her sharp knees and thin skin, and closes her eyes as she catches her breath.

She looks at herself through the front-facing camera on her cell phone, her stomach sinking at the sight of her reflection. She'd applied concealer and a thick layer of foundation before she left the house, but apparently it hadn't been enough to cover the dark circles under her eyes or the hollowness of her cheeks. Her blue dress is too big and hangs awkwardly on her too-small frame. It used to be skin tight. She plays with her hair, trying to hide the ever-growing bald patches that show through her locks, but it's pointless. She puts the phone away and waits for her turn.

"Billie Ouellet?" the nurse calls.

She slowly gets to her feet and follows the woman into the doctor's office. Her steps are slow and laboured, like she's moving through pudding, and all she wants to do is lie down for a nap. She lets the woman weigh her before taking a seat on the examination table.

"Well, look at you!" Dr. Fortin beams, closing the door behind him and taking a seat across from her on the chair. "You're looking so good!"

"Don't."

"Excuse me?"

"Don't lie to me. I look like shit. I'm going bald, my gums are fucking receding from all the vomiting I've done. I can see my ribs and my spine and the fucking divots in my hips. Did you know hips had divots? Because I didn't. But *now* I can fucking measure them. I'm miserable. I want it out."

He opens her file and looks at the notes. "Wow, you're down—"

"One-hundred and sixty-three pounds," she finishes for him. "That's sixty pounds more than you wanted me to lose, and one-hundred and sixty-three pounds more than *I* wanted to. I want it out."

"You want—"

"It. Out," she enunciates slowly. "The Gastra, I want it out. I want it out."

"And what makes you feel this way?"

"I can't eat anything. I can't keep—"

"You knew that portion control was going to be a huge part of the process. Wanting to eat more than you should—"

"I can't eat *anything*! I can't keep it down! I can't eat so much as a fucking steamed carrot without my body violently expelling it from me. And I'm hungry, *so* hungry all the time. Day and night, my stomach is in pain and I'm desperate to eat. But I can't. It's like torture. I've been drinking protein shakes, but they're still coming up if I have too much, or if it's too thick, or if I drink it too fast. I'm miserable. I hate this. *Please*, I need you to take this thing out. It's killing me."

He clicks his tongue against his front teeth, frowning as he flips through her file. "I understand that this has been hard on you. Adjusting to life after bariatric surgery can be tough, and the lifestyle change can be really jarring for some patients, so I get how this has been a struggle for you, I do." He pauses, trying to find a delicate way to word things. "But I also remember you coming to me when you had your stitches taken out and, uh, *exaggerating* a bit, then, too. I think you want this operation to seem harder on you than it actually is because you're looking for an easy way out. And, quite frankly, I don't want to see you undo all your progress because you're a little bit hungry, or feeling too lazy to work out, or because you want to slip into unhealthy habits again. Think about how disappointed you'll be—how disappointed your husband will be—if I let you give up on yourself. So, no, I won't be recommending that we move forward with removing the Gastra-Sphaera GR right now, but if you feel this way at your nine-month follow-up, then we can revisit the idea."

She stares at him in disbelief.

"You just need to trust the process. Okay?"

He doesn't wait for her to answer and instead continues

talking.

She doesn't hear him though. It's like cotton has been stuffed into her ears, or like she's wearing headphones with static blaring in them. All she hears is white noise and the sound of her heart pounding against her ribcage. She doesn't remember the appointment ending, getting into her car, or driving home. And yet, she's aware of herself as she throws her keys on the entranceway table and drops her purse on the rug by the door. She doesn't bother taking her shoes off as she walks into her home, tracking dirt through the hall to the kitchen. She stops in front of the fridge, opens the doors, and looks inside.

Her stomach burns, aching with both hunger and from the weight of the Gastra-Sphaera GR inside of her. She puts her hands on her skin, feeling the hollowness of her body and the bones that stick out from beneath her flesh. She's a skeleton with a pulse, a ghost with a body, a memory of who she used to be. She trails her fingers over her abdomen and stops.

At first, she thinks she's imagining things, that the hunger and emotional exhaustion have gotten to her. But when she runs her hand over her stomach again, she knows she's not crazy: she can feel the Gastra through her skin. She pulls off her dress, letting it fall to the ground, and looks at her stomach. It's concave, except for a small patch that bulges outwards. She pushes her fingers harder against her body, feeling the contour and solidness of the spherical object pushing back from inside her. She hates the device. She hates that it's ruined her life, that it's killing her slowly. She pushes against the Gastra until her nails dig into her waxen skin and come away bloody.

Her stomach growls as her hunger grows.

She looks around the kitchen, fighting through brain fog to figure out which drawer she needs, stumbling unsteadily towards it when she finally remembers. She digs through the drawer, looking for the right tool, and takes out the expensive carving knife she got as a wedding gift. She crosses the room to the dining set, pulls out a chair, and falls into it. She slumps in the seat, making sure she can clearly see the bulge under her skin before she starts.

She pinches the Gastra-Sphaera GR through her skin, steadying it, before taking the knife and pressing it against her skin. She pushes the tip in near her navel and pulls it towards her in a steady motion. Her flesh splits and blood runs out, but she doesn't see the purple shell of the device. She clenches her jaw and repositions the knife, stomach howling with hunger, and she pushes deeper as she retraces the first cut. There's an audible scraping of the metal against a hard surface, and she smiles. She lets the knife fall out of her hand and onto the ground before reaching into the incision and gripping the Gastra-Sphaera GR with her bare hand. She pulls, smiling as she hears the wet tearing of the device being unsewn from her stomach. She loses her grip, the wet device slippery in her hand, and exhales with frustration. She plunges her fingers back into the wound, makes a fist around the Gastra, and gives it one more hard pull.

With a loud squelch, it pops out.

Billie rolls it between her fingers, looking at the purple sphere, still heavy with solution, and tosses it onto the table. It rolls off the edge and onto the floor, but she doesn't bother to pick it up. She's given it enough of her attention and refuses to give it a second more.

She gets up out of the wooden chair and crosses the room, her hunger propelling her forward, taking care not to slip in the blood that coats her legs and drips onto the floor. She opens the fridge and pulls out the first Tupperware she sees, rips the lid off, and shovels a handful of the food into her mouth. She chews fast and swallows, relief washing over her when the food doesn't come back up.

She doesn't notice the masticated chicken as it spills out of the wound in her abdomen or the splatter of it hitting the tile.

She just smiles and takes another bite.

TEETH

I'm shedding my teeth.

My beautiful, $7000 teeth.
The ones that hide behind my lips,
and deep in the black of my mouth
each time I'm told to smile.

Words will feel too big,
or not big enough,
in the hollow of my cheek.

They'll feel rough, and soft,
and taste artificial
—like sweetener—
without my rows of ivory shieldmen.

My tongue will mourn its polite outlet for noise,
its clicking in quiet passive aggression,
as big words are made small
and explained back to me.

Lines of white replaced with pink flesh
that bleeds and breaks
when I'd rather eat glass
than grin and bear it.

I'm shedding the teeth I cut on being nice.

Now, I'm sharpening my tongue.

THE ONLY THING TO FEAR

Gwen pulls the flyer off of her locker and frowns. It's the same as all the other ones that have been posted around the school: a duck-egg blue background, the darkened silhouette of a teen mid transformation, and bright pineapple yellow words scrawled across the top. 'THE ONLY THING TO FEAR IS SHAME ITSELF!' the paper reads in a thick marker font. She rolls her eyes at the date written at the bottom of the poster and waves the paper in her friend's face.

"Are they *really* making us all go to this assembly today?"

"Technically, it's two assemblies—the juniors are having theirs this morning and we get ours this afternoon—but yes."

"Ugh," Gwen grumbles, spinning the dial of the lock clockwise. "It's so boring. It's not like we don't already know about this stuff. Mr. Ryan gives the same speech every single year. We practically know it by heart."

Roisin leans against a nearby locker with a smile, tucking a strand of her curly red hair behind her pierced ear and peering at her friend through her lashes. "I, for one, am excited for today's assembly."

"That's because you get to skip French, which you suck at."

"*Bien sûr, mon amie,*" she laughs.

"Think there's a way I can sit it out?" Gwen asks, rummaging through her as she looks for her math books.

"Now why would you want to do that?" asks a voice from behind her. Arms wrap around her waist and hug her from behind, and a kiss is planted on the back of her shoulder.

"Not only do we get to miss the boring lecture on Sappho, but we can sit in the back of the auditorium and spend the entire assembly making out."

"Wow, Mateo, that sounds like so much fun," Roisin says drily, crossing her arms in front of her chest, her smile no longer reaching her eyes.

"Don't worry, you're not invited."

Gwen turns to smile at her boyfriend, dislodging herself from his grasp. "I have a feeling Ms. Rileigh is going to make us sit with the rest of class."

"A man can dream."

"And that's all he can do," Roisin mutters under her breath.

Mateo glares at her before turning his attention back to Gwen. "Anyway, I've gotta run. I'll see you in English." He leans in and kisses her quickly on the lips before she can pull away. "I can't wait for tonight."

He waves to Gwen before turning his attention to the gaggle of boys down the hall, and she lets out the breath she'd been holding

"You're seeing him tonight?"

"Uh, yeah. We're just gonna hang out and watch movies."

"Mhm."

"Did you want to come over too?"

Roisin's laugh is more like a bark. "I'd rather eat glass. Besides, I don't think I'm invited. He's never liked me." Gwen opens her mouth to disagree, but she hates lying to her friend, so she closes it without saying anything. "I thought you were going to break up with him? What was it you said? 'He's definitely not my type,' wasn't it?"

"I don't know. I was thinking about it. What we have right now is fine…"

"But?"

"…but he keeps pushing for more, and I guess I'm not ready for it."

"You're not ready for more, or you're not ready for

more *from him*?"

"I don't want to talk about it."

"Gwen—"

"I don't want to talk about it." Gwen shuts the door with a sigh, hooking the combination lock through the metal loop and snapping the shackle closed.

"Whatever," Roisin says, heading lazily to class. "Come on, we're going to be late for math."

Gwen spins the dial on her lock one more time and follows after her friend.

"I just don't get why we keep calling them werewolves when they're not werewolves," the blonde girl says with an exaggerated sigh. Her friends in the row beside her snicker, as do some of the boys sitting behind her. Gwen rolls her eyes at the question and shifts in her seat. Mateo's hand is hot on her thigh, and she wants nothing more than to swat it away. He looks at her with a smile, so she smiles back and puts her hand on top of his.

"Well, they're not called werewolves," Mr. Ryan—the school's senior-most health and wellness teacher—answers irritably. "They're called loups-garous or rougarous, and wolves have nothing to do with it. Every transformation looks different, even if they do all happen between dusk and dawn. Some people have canine-like features, while others resemble boars, owls, or even cats. Remember, we're trying to end the stigma surrounding loups-garous, especially when two out of every five students your age will experience an outbreak. Perpetuating this werewolf—this *monster*—stereotype only does more harm than good. When we're talking about loups-garous, what's the most dangerous thing?"

"Shame!" the audience yells back at him, well rehearsed in this speech. Gwen stays quiet and crosses one leg over the other, hoping the change will dissuade Mateo from keeping his hand on her.

Success!

He takes his hand off her leg and instead leans towards her, wrapping an arm around her shoulders. She's somehow made the situation worse.

"Exactly. It's why establishing healthy relationships with your family and friends is so important during your high school and college years. Because while adult outbreaks are still common—one in six adults will have at least one experience of turning into a loup-garou between the ages of 25 and 65, and one in eight will continue to experience outbreaks well into retirement—they impact almost *half* the population during adolescence."

Mr. Ryan takes a seat on the edge of the stage, his white sneakers squeaking against the wood as he arranges himself more comfortably. His green tracksuit with the school's logo— a knight holding a lance and a shield—blends into the background, painted the same green with the same logo. He carelessly bangs the microphone against the floor, staff and students cringing from the loud noise, before turning his attention back to the audience to answer the same questions he gets every school year.

"Yes, Geoffrey?"

"Is it true we have to draw blood *and* recognize the person to cure them from being a rougarou? 'Cause, like, bruh, I don't want to hurt my friend." People around the auditorium laugh, including Mateo. Gwen doesn't get what's so funny.

"No, that's just another misconception, much like the one that becoming a loup-garou happens when you miss Easter for seven years or fail to observe lent. Undergoing the transformation only happens to students who are dealing with immense shame. A shame that's so bad they don't feel like themselves anymore. For some people, that comes with neglecting religious duties, for others it's not getting straight As. So the best thing you can do for someone dealing with shame is?"

"To love them!" the room echoes back.

"Exactly! To love them! If your friend is dealing with shame, you hopefully wouldn't want to punch them, you'd want to be there for them. You'd want them to know they're not alone and that you see them for who they really are. It's the same with a loup-garou transformation. If you see someone?"

"Tell someone!" they reply in unison.

Mateo leans in and kisses Gwen on the cheek and she turns her attention away from the assembly. He moves quickly, finding her lips in the dark before she realizes he's trying to make out with her. She puts a hand on his chest to push him away, but he mistakes it for a romantic gesture and puts his hand over hers.

Behind them, their teacher clears her throat loudly, and Mateo sighs, turning his attention back to Mr. Ryan. Gwen exhales loudly, knowing he'll interpret it as shared disappointment and not the relief she feels. She looks out into the sea of faces and spots Roisin looking back at her. Her friend jumps in her seat slightly, and turns back to watch Mr. Ryan before Gwen can wave to her. Even from across the room, Gwen's surprised at how red her friend's ears seem to have turned.

"Exactly!" Mr. Ryan is saying with forced enthusiasm. "If you see someone, tell someone! Studies show that unreported loups-garous sightings usually lead to a spike of cases, so do your part to prevent outbreaks. Not to mention, as we all know, the only way to stop the loup-garou condition is to recognize the person who's been transformed. So if *you* don't recognize the loup-garou, that doesn't mean someone else won't!"

"Okay, but like, nobody wants to get caught being a loup-garou," the same blonde girl says. Although she directs the comment to one of her friends, it's loud enough for the rest of the room to hear. "I think I'd die of embarrassment if someone caught me rutting around the mall with a pig's nose and a curly tail."

From across the room someone snorts while pretending to ask a store clerk if jeggings are half off. It's not especially funny, but it's enough to send the immature students into hysterics. Mr. Ryan sighs loudly into the mic as the teachers try to get their classes under control.

It's going to be a very long afternoon for all of them.

Mateo runs his hand over the top of Gwen's thigh and her entire body tenses up. When he'd invited her over to "chill," Gwen had been led to believe that his parents were going to be there too. He'd made it sound like all of them would be spending the afternoon loafing on the couch watching old horror movies and passing around Jiffy Pop popcorn and gummy worms. Instead, she was alone with him in his too-big house and searching for any excuse to leave.

"Uh, this is a really good part," she says, pulling away from him and nodding to the TV. Her hands are balled into fists, which she keeps glued to her sides, and she finds it hard to meet Mateo's gaze.

"Mmm, yeah," he whispers, "this *is* a really good part."

He trails his hand up her thigh a little higher and moves his body even closer to hers, nibbling at her neck. He slips a hand under her shirt, placing it on her stomach, and it feels painfully hot against her skin. Then he starts sliding it up.

"Ohmygod, no," she says, pushing him back and leaping to her feet.

"What? Why?"

"I'm not ready."

"What do you mean you're not ready? You seemed like you were totally into this."

"I'm not, I'm really *really* not."

"Babe," he says looking up at her from his spot on the couch, "come sit back down. We can take it slower." When she hesitates, he pouts and taps the space next to him. "Please?"

She sits down on the couch, leaving a cushion between them, and tries to focus on the television. But before a full five minutes have passed, he's pressed up against her and kissing a trail up to her ear.

"Okay, no! What did I *literally* just say?" She gets up again and crosses the room, throwing on her jacket and picking up her purse from its spot on the recliner.

"You said you wanted to take it slow! I was taking it slow!"

"Yeah, well now I don't want you taking it anywhere."

"What the hell's your problem? We've been dating for like three months now and we haven't done anything. You don't want to make out with me, you don't want me to touch you, like? Why are you even dating me?"

The question catches her off guard and makes her angry. She's about to say something cruel, but the pained look on his face curbs some of her fury. A long minute goes by before she answers him honestly.

"I just wanted to feel normal. I'm sorry."

Before he can ask any follow-up questions, she heads into the entranceway and pulls on her shoes before leaving his house and slipping into the night.

At first Gwen thinks it's her imagination acting up, since she hardly slept the night before. Although she tried to squeeze some sleep in before her alarm was set to go off, she spent most of that time awake and worried, trying to imagine how uncomfortable the rest of the semester would be. She only shares two classes with Mateo, but he's a popular guy and has friends in all her other courses, and she can't help but fret that school is suddenly about to get complicated for her. Midterms are behind them, which means finals and (hopefully) college are just around the corner. She doesn't need to worry about her ex-boyfriend, she needs to worry about grades. But when a group of girls from her gym class stops talking just long enough for her to walk by, she knows something's wrong.

People are talking about her.

Eyes follow her as she walks down the hall and opens her locker. As she sorts through her books and stores her finished homework in the correct binders, she becomes acutely aware that people aren't just talking about her. They're laughing.

"Have a fun night last night?" a girl asks a few lockers down.

"Uh, not especially." It's an innocent enough answer, but it elicits cackling from the students listening to the exchange.

"You know, that's exactly what Mateo told us. Well, texted us."

"What do you mean?"

"Don't worry, practice makes perfect." For some reason they also find this hilarious, and they take off down the hall.

Gwen holds her binder and textbook in one arm, shoves her backpack into the locker, and closes it loudly before heading off to her first class. People continue to stare as she heads to World History, and more than one student asks if she'd "like to practice" with them. With every "no" and with increased bewilderment from Gwen, the joke gets funnier for everyone else, and by the time she's sitting in the back corner of the classroom she's feeling close to tears. It's only when Roisin takes a seat next to her that a wave of relief hits Gwen.

But it's short lived.

Roisin stares into her notebook, face flushed, and ignores Gwen's greeting. It's only when the teacher comes in and begins the lecture that she finally looks up from her notes and stares dead ahead. Gwen spends most of the hour trying to get her friend's attention, but her efforts go ignored and unnoticed. When the bell finally rings, Roisin rushes to leave the room, but Gwen grabs her by the arm and pulls her back.

"What the hell?" she cries. "Everyone's been treating me like shit all morning, and you don't want to talk to me? Why? What the hell did I do?"

"Mateo," she says drily.

"What? I thought you'd be happy about that. I mean, I know I should have texted you sooner about it, but like—"

"*Why* would *I* be happy about that?"

"Because you hated him, or at least you acted like it. I thought you'd be thrilled we broke up."

Roisin's head snaps up at this comment, finally meeting Gwen's gaze. "You did what now?"

"I broke up with Mateo. Isn't that what you just said you were mad about?"

Roisin bites her lip and looks down at the floor before exhaling hard. "Oh man, no, that's definitely not what I meant. Gwen, there's a rumour going around that, uh, he broke up with you—"

She rolls her eyes and cuts off her friend. "Of course there is. Whatever, I really can't be bothered with—"

"—because you were bad in bed," she finishes.

Gwen's mouth is suddenly dry and her chest hurts. "He said I was bad in bed?"

Roisin's ears get red and she suddenly can't look at Gwen anymore. "So you *did* sleep with him then?"

"I think I'm going to be sick."

Gwen pushes past Roisin, who calls after her, and she rushes back to her locker. She throws her binder in and grabs her backpack, slamming the door behind her. She runs through the halls and out the front door, the whispers and laughs following her home.

She sits on the edge of her bed, opening and closing her hands, the long nails biting into her palm each time. When she got home, she threw up in the entranceway of her house, cleaning it up before her parents got in from work. She then spent the rest of the day locked in her bedroom, saying she wanted to be alone and insisting it was just period cramps when her family came to check on her. She couldn't tell them about the rumour going around the school. She couldn't tell them about a lot of things. Eventually the afternoon faded into the evening, and by the time the sun had fully set she had transformed into her other self. Her hideous self.

Although Mr. Ryan had told the assembly that wolves had little to do with loups-garous, her body had clearly missed the memo. Although she'd never quite cleared five feet when human, she now stood almost seven feet tall, her healthy frame made lean by the extra height. The short brown hair that covered her head now trailed down her chest and her back, and darkened her forearms. Her hands grew bony and her knuckles more pronounced, and her short nails had been replaced by long claws. In this form, her clothing didn't fit, so she fashioned herself a makeshift toga from a bedsheet and belt. She ran a hand across her snout, nose long and mouth wide with pointed teeth, and she tried to choke back the bile she felt creeping up the back of her throat as she looked at herself in the mirror. When she'd first turned into a loup-garou months earlier, the transformation had only been a curse. It was just one more thing to feel ashamed of.

Now, thinking of Mateo and the pain she was eager to inflict, she wonders if it could possibly be a gift. Mr. Ryan had said the most dangerous thing about her kind is shame. She disagrees. She thinks it's the razor-sharp appendages.

She opens the bedroom window and steps delicately onto the roof, careful to shut the sliding glass quietly behind her. She tiptoes across the shingles, not wanting to wake up the family dog, before making her way onto the nearby tree branch and climbing down the sturdy maple. Her father has always joked that he should cut down that tree to keep her safe from future boyfriends. Maybe he should have cut it down to keep exes safe from her.

She crosses the manicured lawn, the wet grass squishing under her bare feet, her unnaturally long legs helping her move faster than she normally would. Although she hates turning into a monster every night, the physical advantages that come with it are plenty. Her gym class is an exercise in exhaustion and physical ineptitude, but in her loup-garou form she has boundless energy and stamina. It's what normally keeps her up all night and it's what propels her forward now. She sprints down the dimly lit streets, hoping people are asleep and can't see her, or are too tired to notice or care. The last thing she needs now is for someone to spot her and for her school to find out she's a beast.

As she approaches the fence around Mateo's house, her stomach begins to churn and her skin feels hot with betrayal. She knows she hurt him, made him feel unwanted, but what he did? That was unforgivable. Cruel. The way they'd all laughed at her. The way they'd all spoken about her.

The way Roisin had looked at her.

Just the thought of it makes her want to shred Mateo to ribbons.

She hopes her ex is good at reading expressions, since loups-garous are notoriously mute, but she thinks she'd be willing to write her grievances in his flesh if push came to shove.

As she stands outside the fence she hears rustling behind her. At first, Gwen thinks it's an animal, but then the steps get louder and she realizes she's not alone. She turns on her heel, caught off guard, and finds another loup-garou behind her in the grass. The creature is taller than her and sports a long wiry tail. The fur that covers its face is copper and shines like fire under the light of the moon. The creature's bright green eyes widen in surprise and it lets out a little gasp.

Roisin?

Gwen? The girls think simultaneously.

The air around them changes. Whatever fury and violence brought Gwen to Mateo's yard is released suddenly, like air rushing from a balloon. The two of them stare at each other, transfixed, as the hair vanishes, their bones shorten, and their claws retract. The transformation is over in a matter of seconds, and two barefoot girls wrapped in bedsheets stand where the monsters once stood.

"What the hell are you doing here?" Roisin asks.

"Me? What the hell are *you* doing here? And you're a loup-garou? Since when? Why didn't you tell me?"

"Asked pot to kettle," she snaps. "You first!"

"Okay, uh, well, I was here to kick Mateo's ass."

"Really?"

"Yeah. Maybe more," Gwen admits, pulling the blanket tight around her shoulders. "I was pissed! He lied to the school. We never, you know…"

"I know."

"You do?"

Roisin stares at the ground and runs a hand through her hair. "After you left, I spoke to him—"

"Spoke?"

She smiles sheepishly. "Okay, I screamed at him. He told me what happened, that he was pissed, and that he made everything up. And when he refused to tell everyone the truth… I don't know. I thought maybe I could intimidate him into admitting he lied."

"You were going to do that for me?"

Roisin shrugs, blushing. "Yeah, of course. I'd do anything for you."

"Why didn't you tell me you were a loup-garou?" Gwen asks.

"I don't know. I guess I didn't want to ruin our friendship," Roisin admits.

"You thought I'd stop being your friend if you told me you were a loup-garou?"

"No, of course not! It's just… it's complicated."

"Have you been one for long?"

"A year," she says, looking around the empty yard. "I take it this is a new experience for you, courtesy of Mateo?"

Gwen shakes her head, finding it hard to look Roisin in the eyes. "A couple of months."

"What?" Roisin cries. "Why didn't you tell me?"

"I don't know. I guess for the same reason you didn't want to tell me."

With one last look behind her, Gwen turns away from Mateo's house and starts heading back the way she came, Roisin walking beside her.

"I can't believe you recognized me," Gwen admits, shivering in the cold air.

"I'd know your moody stance anywhere. I'm actually surprised you could tell who I was with those whiskers."

"You mean those ginger whiskers?" Gwen laughs, reaching out to tuck a lock of Roisin's hair behind her ear. "You could shave your head and I'd still recognize that melon."

The two of them chuckle under the moon as they make their way through the maze of quiet streets.

"So what's the big secret?" Roisin eventually asks as Gwen's house comes into view.

"Oh, uh, maybe let's save that for another night?"

"Mr. Ryan says if you don't spill the beans after someone recognizes you, then the shame will just turn you back again."

"The only thing to fear is shame itself," Gwen imitates.

"Exactly. Might as well rip this Band-Aid off while we're here."

"Only if you say yours too."

The two of them stand close to each other under a streetlamp, shivering from both the cold and their nerves. Gwen's stomach does backflips while Roisin plays compulsively with her hair.

"Same time?" Roisin suggests.

Gwen nods.

"One," says Roisin.

"Two," continues Gwen.

"Three."

"I have a crush on you," they say in unison.

The silence between them grows and expands. At first it feels like it's going to consume them both, but then, just as suddenly, it's gone. Relief and disbelief floods them, and before they know it they're laughing together in the starlight.

"I don't know if I should be happy or terrified," Roisin

admits.

"Both. Definitely both."

"So then did you, uh, I don't know, want to hang out or something?" she asks, shifting her weight back and forth on her feet, the pavement rough under her smooth skin.

"We hang out all the time. Take me on a date," Gwen says sheepishly.

Roisin closes the distance between them and pecks Gwen on the cheek, a smile growing on her face as she pulls away. "I'll see what I can do."

"Get home safe," Gwen says.

Roisin waves a shy farewell and Gwen watches her walk away into the night, staring into the distance long after she's faded from view.

As she heads back to her house, she can't help but chuckle. Maybe Mr. Ryan was right after all.

LLANWEY POINT

She peruses the row of snacks, trying to strike a balance between what she wants and what she knows will fuel her body for the day of hiking that awaits her. She ends up settling on a box of protein bars, but she also grabs a bag of chocolate-covered almonds to satisfy her sweet tooth. At the back of the shop, she opens one of the glass doors, the icy refrigerator air chilling her skin and giving her goosebumps, and takes one of the VitaminWaters off the shelf.

"You know we have food in the cooler, right?" Daniel says from behind her.

"Yeah, but I'm not in the mood for any of it, so I want to grab a few small things before we get going, you know?"

"You do realize the more you buy the more you have to carry, right?"

"No, the more I buy the more *you* have to carry since you're the one lugging the cooler."

"Like hell I do," he laughs.

The two of them browse a bit more, their hiking shoes tapping obnoxiously against the tiled floor of the convenience store. The fluorescent lights are on overhead, but the sunlight streaming in through the windows is stronger and steeps everything in a warm yellow glow. Rebecca gets distracted at the magazine stand, eyeing the newest tabloids with curiosity, before letting Daniel lead her away. They head down the last of the small rows, remembering to grab a bottle of sunscreen and some bug repellent, before heading to the front of the store to pay.

"Hello!" the elderly woman behind the counter says with a smile. She enters each item number into the register, the keys clicking softly beneath her wrinkled hands, the outdated machine whirring. She holds up the sunscreen while she keys in the price. "It's a beautiful day to be going outside," she says cheerily, putting the plastic bottle into a paper bag with the rest of the goods.

"Isn't it?" Rebecca chirps.

"Where are you two going?"

"Llanwey Point! His dad," she gestures to Daniel, who shifts uncomfortably from foot to foot as she speaks, "used to take him camping there when he was young and now he's taking me for our anniversary."

The woman raises an eyebrow. "Llanwey Point?"

"Yeah, have you heard of it?"

"Oh, I'm sure she's heard of it," Daniel interjects. "It's really nothing special."

"Then why are you taking me?" she laughs.

"Well, I mean, it's special *to me* and I'm sure you'll love it. But it's really not a touristy spot or anything."

"That's because it's in the middle of nowhere," the woman says. She presses a button on the cash register and there's a loud click as it displays the total owed. "It's a hard spot to get to if you're not used to trekking through the woods, and there's not much to do once you get there."

"Really?"

"Mhmm. Talbot's Ridge is a bit closer and it's a pretty gorgeous place this time of year, even with all the tourists, and it'll give you a better view of the land than the Point will."

"Well, maybe next time," Daniel says, passing the woman a few bills and taking the paper bag off the counter.

"Of course," she says pleasantly, opening the cash drawer and getting his change. "Be careful though. We've had a bit of a wildlife problem in these parts this past month. At first, we thought it was coyotes because a few house cats went missing, but someone claimed it was a pack of wolves who were getting too comfortable around humans. I know the rangers have been keeping an eye on the situation, but better safe than sorry."

Daniel raises his eyebrow and leans against the counter. "Wolves, eh?"

The woman nods her head sadly. "That's one possibility the Rangers are considering, although they still haven't ruled out the coyotes. A family was out for a hike and they saw a group of *something* in the woods with them. The two kids said they saw a massive wolf, but the parents say coyotes, so who knows?"

"They probably saw the alpha," Dnaiel says excitedly.

"Maybe," the woman says, "or something pretending to be one. Wolves will normally avoid people and aren't usually aggressive, so it makes me wonder what's getting them to act unnaturally like that." She shrugs, seemingly to herself. "Maybe I'm just being paranoid, though. Still, you might want to make some noise and keep to the trails to be on the safe side."

Rebecca nods. "Absolutely. Thanks for the heads up."

She waves to the old woman and follows Daniel out of the shop.

"I don't want to be 'that guy,' but are we almost there yet?" she asks, stopping momentarily to catch her breath.

Daniel shakes his head, looking at the small map for a moment before folding it back up and shoving it in the back pocket of his cargo pants. "No, we're not going to be there for a while. It's like a six-hour hike *if* we don't stop for breaks. And you've been needing a rest practically every hour."

She shakes her head in disbelief. "You must have been one extremely fit kid. I feel like I'm going to fucking die."

"It'll be worth it, I promise."

She takes her water bottle out of her backpack's side pocket, unfastens the cap, and takes a swig. It's cold and crisp and she immediately feels renewed as she gulps it back, glad she splurged on the massive bottle before agreeing to go on this trip with him.

"Ready?" he asks, apparently desperate to keep

moving up the hill.

"What's so special about this place, anyway?" Rebecca asks.

"It's just a really nice spot that my dad used to take me to."

"Yeah?"

"Yeah."

"Like, a spot nice enough to take *our* kids, one day?"

He clicks his tongue against the back of his teeth and turns his back to her, resting his hands on the top of his head as he exhales loudly.

"Are we really doing this again?" he asks, voice loud and deep. "Are we really having this conversation again?"

"I guess not," Rebecca says, voice getting stuck in the back of her throat.

"You know how I feel about that."

"Yeah," she says through clenched teeth, "I do."

She puts the lid back on her water bottle and slips it back into the pocket of her bag. It's heavy, and though she's glad to have it, she's unenthusiastic about having to drag around the weight of it for the next few hours. Overhead, the clouds look thicker and grey, the sun from earlier that morning beginning to fade and move behind them. They walk in silence for what feels like ages, before Rebecca feels like she can talk again.

"Why do you want to go now?"

"What do you mean?"

"Well, it's just, I don't know, it feels weird. Like, I've heard you actively complain about camping and how you think it's dumb to sleep outside when you have a perfectly comfortable house. But now you're dragging me through the woods at the first chance you get to revisit some secret childhood family camping spot. Except you've literally never mentioned it before last week. It just seems weird, I guess."

"I've mentioned it before," he argues halfheartedly.

"No, you haven't, or at least not to me."

"I'm pretty sure I've mentioned it before."

"No, definitely not. There's a lot you don't tell me, apparently."

"Rebecca—"

"Whatever. All I'm saying is that it was only after you did that weird ancestry project on your grandfather—"

"Great-grandfather—"

"—that you ever brought the place up."

The two of them continue to make their way through the forest, following the signposts that have been laid out for tourists. Although most of them point the way to Talbot's Ridge, a few of the signs point them in the direction of Llanwey Point.

"I don't know," Daniel says slowly, trying to get the words right. "My dad used to take me there when I was younger. He was always looking for something and I guess I never understood what that was until recently."

"And what exactly was it?"

"To find where he belongs."

The sky grows dark overhead and Rebecca grows more tired with each step. She hasn't walked this long uphill in forever, and she dreads the thought of having to make her way back down from Llanwey Point. The woods are quiet and she realizes that, for the first time since they left that morning, the only thing she can hear is their footsteps on the path. The birds, the insects, and even the trees have fallen silent. Something moves behind her, silent as fog, but when she turns to see what it is, it's gone.

"I don't like this," she admits out loud.

"Don't like what?" Daniel asks.

"This forest. It's too quiet." A shiver passes through her. "I feel like I'm being watched."

"Aren't all forests like that?"

"Not really. Maybe we should turn back. Something

doesn't feel right."

"Don't be stupid, it's fine."

"Excuse me?" Her voice is sharp, an octave higher than normal, offended by his choice of words.

"Sorry, I don't mean it like that, just… I'm not turning back. Not when we're so close."

"Why do you always treat me like shit?"

"I don't always treat you like shit, stop exaggerating."

"There you go again."

Daniel shakes his head, refusing to look at her as he moves through the green.

"So what are we close to, exactly? The random sense of belonging your great-grandpa found? This is bullshit," she snaps.

Daniel doesn't reply.

"Sorry," she apologizes after a moment, letting out a sigh. "I'm not trying to be mean, I'm just frustrated with everything. With *us*. And I just don't get what this big revelation was, or what you're after."

Daniel walks down the path, silent, and Rebecca wonders if he's even going to answer her. Just when she thinks he's going to give her the silent treatment for the rest of the trip, he speaks again.

"My dad told me, when I was a kid, that his grandfather had never really fit in with other people. But after he came to Llanwey Point, he understood who he really was and came to realize that he didn't fit in with people because he wasn't like everyone else. He was special."

"How so?"

"He just… was. Unfortunately, he died not long after coming out to Llanwey and I always just assumed my dad had been making shit up because our family history was so boring."

"But he wasn't?"

Daniel shakes his head. "Apparently not. I was able to get in touch with some of the people who'd heard of my great-grandfather or whose parents or family knew him. People who'd lived in the area but had moved away after his death. They seemed to back the stories my dad had been telling for years."

"So if you know that your dad wasn't lying—"

"If he's telling the truth, it's one I need to know for myself."

He walks faster now, branches swinging dangerously behind him as he pushes through the thick of the trees. The sun is gone from view and the wind picks up. Rebecca wants to pry, but thunder roars overhead and the hill starts to get steeper. She tries not to worry about the strange tone in Daniel's voice and keeps moving.

She stands at the base of the footpath, the wind whipping her hair and howling through the trees as she looks over her shoulder and back the way they came. The back of her neck prickles and her hair stands on end.

"Are you coming?" Daniel asks impatiently, ahead of her on the trail.

Rebecca looks back at him and then shines her flashlight on the ground before her. The earth is cracked and littered with tree roots, stones, and tufts of grass that all look poised to trip her up and twist her ankles. The sky is dark and the clouds are thick with rain, the humidity making her clothing stick to her damp skin. It's early evening, according to her watch, but it feels like midnight.

"Yeah, I guess… it's just, isn't there another way up?"

"No."

"Well then, maybe we should wait until morning? We can set up camp around here and then make the trek up tomorrow?"

"Why would we wait when we can do it now?" he asks, doing nothing to mask the annoyance that creeps into his voice.

"Because it seems dangerous. It's hard to see the trail and I'm worried that—"

"That's what flashlights are for."

"Yeah, I know, but I just—"

"Come on!" Daniel calls before turning his back to her and continuing up the hill.

She follows him reluctantly, checking over her shoulder as she climbs the narrow path, branches scratching at her face and catching in her hair. It feels like the forest is trying to grab her, like the very trees are trying to hook themselves into her skin and stop her from making her ascent. Something moves behind her in the dark—it's the same thing that's been following her all day, appearing at the edges of her vision and disappearing before she can register what it is—and she forces herself to move faster.

Her legs shake with exhaustion as she reaches the top of the hill. Thunder crashes overhead, but the rain doesn't fall. The wind is stronger up here, colder, and she wraps her arms around herself as it pierces her sweat-dampened skin like shards of ice. Her teeth chatter and she shivers, shining her flashlight through the darkness as she tries to find Daniel. She is about to call out his name, nervous at being left alone, but she spots him past the edge of the woods in a small clearing. It takes her a while to catch up, her legs shorter and slower than his, but eventually she meets him in the empty space atop Llanwey Point.

"We should get the tent set up," she says, throwing her backpack and sleeping bag onto the ground next to the cooler and the rest of Daniel's belongings. "It looks like it's going to piss pour rain. The tent is waterproof, right?"

Daniel isn't listening to her. He's too busy looking out into the black around them, watching the shapes move in the trees, almost imperceivable to the naked eye. But he's been waiting for them, hoping for them, and now that they're here he's almost too excited to think. She says something, but he doesn't hear it.

"Daniel?" She calls his name louder now.

"What?"

"Is the tent waterproof?" she asks, rifling through the things on the ground. She shines her light on the packs, heart sinking when she doesn't find it.

"I didn't bring a tent."

"You forgot the fucking tent?" she asks in disbelief.

"I didn't forget it, I just didn't bring it."

"*Why*?"

"Because we don't need it, Rebecca. We don't need any of the shit we brought. Not anymore."

He looks into the sea of green that surrounds them and smiles.

"What are you *talking* about?" she asks, frustrated. "It's going to storm and we're like eight fucking hours from anything. Why, *why* wouldn't you bring a tent with you?"

"Because we don't *need* it. We don't need anything now."

"What the fuck does that even mean?" she gets up off her knees and points the flashlight in the direction they came from. "I'm going back. If we go now, the trees might give us enough shelter from the rain that we won't be soaking wet by the time we get back to the car."

"Rebecca, we don't need to go back. We just need to be patient and let them do their thing."

"Let *who* do *what*?"

Daniel points to the treeline and she watches the branches shake and move. At first, she thinks it's the wind from the impending storm, but then she sees the shadows moving slowly through the woods. They've been dancing in her blindspot all day, but now she can see them clearly as they move together.

Wolves.

They move slowly towards the clearing, keeping their backs to the edge of the trees. They look exactly like she remembers from nature shows and from the zoos her parents took her to when she was younger. Each one is about four feet long and two feet tall with eyes that glow in the darkness.

Rebecca shines her flashlight at one of them and realizes why people have been confused about whether they had seen wolves or coyotes: their fur is a mix of rust red and mud brown, with patches of grey and white colouring their underbellies and legs. From a distance, it would be easy to confuse the pack of red wolves for coyotes.

One of the animals steps out from behind the trees and begins to move closer. This creature is bigger than the others, with silver fur and eyes that glow green in the dead of night. There's no mistaking this animal for anything other than a wolf, and she shivers as it watches her.

"Daniel," she whispers, backing up towards him. "Daniel, we need to go. We need to get the fuck out of here."

"Calm down," he breathes excitedly as he runs his hands through his hair and fiddles with his shirt. "This is what we came for. This is what *I* came for."

"To get fucking eaten by wolves?" she hisses.

"To belong."

The giant wolf moves forward and Rebecca takes a step back.

"Stop moving," Daniel snaps. "This is what we came for."

He holds his arms out wide, like he's preparing to give someone a bear hug, and stands perfectly still as all the wolves begin to move forward.

"Daniel," Rebecca screams, "we need to go right fucking now!"

He turns to face her, furious. "Don't you fucking dare! I didn't come all this way to chicken out. *You* didn't come all this way to chicken out. Just stay still and let them bite you."

"*What*?" she gaps, disbelieving.

"It's okay! They'll bite us and we'll become like them. We'll become part of their pack. Just like my great-grandfather was."

"Are you fucking nuts?" she yells, trying to move away without spurring the animals into an attack.

"My dad wanted this for me too, wanted this for

himself, but the wolves never came for him. I guess he didn't have what it takes to join them. But I do. *We* do."

"*We?*" she shouts, the words bursting out of her mouth before she can silence them.

"Think about it, Rebecca. This is your chance to have the family you wanted. The family *you* asked for."

Rebecca shakes her head and shines the flashlight on the woods behind her. "I didn't ask for this. I never asked for this!" She sees the footpath they took up the hill and, before she can change her mind or lose her nerve, she runs for it.

That's all it takes for the wolves to spring into action. The grass crunches behind her and the ground shakes from their paws on the cold ground, charging towards where she was standing. Rebecca runs as fast as her legs will take her, but soon she hears the footsteps of a beast close behind and gaining on her. She hears the bite before she feels it, a wet tear that pierces the woods around her, and then she screams at the heat that consumes her arm from elbow to thumb as she drops the flashlight. She looks down and screams again at the exposed bone, the muscle and flesh ripped away. The massive silver wolf passes her and blocks her way back down the hill. It watches her with green eyes that see through her and she cries from the pain and the terror as she turns back the way she came.

The other wolves run around the clearing, making circles in the grass around Daniel as he stands with his arms outstretched, confused. She trips over one of the discarded bags on the ground beside him and falls to her knees next to him, holding her bloody arm close to her chest. Rebecca pulls out her phone and tries to dial 9-1-1, but Daniel slaps the phone out of her hand, stopping her from pressing send.

"What are you doing?" she sobs. The animals watch as they run circles around them, the massive wolf slowly coming into view from the footpath.

"You don't need it," he says, nodding to the wolves. "You're changing, healing. See?"

The throbbing in Rebecca's arm begins to dull and

tingle, and she watches with horror as her muscle slowly grows back and the flesh knits itself together, leaving behind a pale thin scar to mark where the wound had been. She looks at her arm, fascinated as she opens and closes her hand, testing the new flesh.

"Told you," Daniel says, shifting his attention from her and back to the wolves.

Suddenly, a spasm runs through her body. She feels like she's been touched with a live wire as her skin grows hot and her muscles clench. Her arms begin to grey and darken as fur begins to sprout from the newly mended skin, spreading and growing across her entire body. She screams as her bones begin to shift and move inside her, widening and lengthening as she changes shape. Her spine feels like it's being put through a taffy puller as her coccyx lengthens into a tail, and her mouth feels like it's being torn open as her face and jaw stretch into a snout. She wants to scream and cry and beg for the pain to stop, but all she can do is howl and whine. Eventually, her body is quiet and she opens her eyes, unsure of when she closed them, and sees the world for the first time.

Daniel stands in the center of the wolf pack, arms by his side, face glistening with sweat. He stares back at her and she realizes that his heart is beating fast enough that she can hear it beneath his skin. Even in complete darkness, she can see the lines of worry and confusion etched on his face.

The silver wolf approaches Rebecca and her body reacts on its own, hackles raised, teeth exposed, fur on edge. The beast moves closer, undeterred, and rubs his face against hers, sniffing the air. He lets out a whoop and a howl, the other wolves stopping in their tracks and making their way to their new sister. They run excited circles around her and she can't help but revel in the shared enthusiasm of her pack.

Of her family.

The wolves make their way to the tree line, the silver werewolf following after them. Daniel stands still in the clearing, watching them go, before turning to Rebecca. He holds out his arm, expectantly, waiting for her to share this new gift with him.

"Come on!" he shouts at her, waving his arm towards her. "It's my turn."

The silver beast watches her from the trees, waiting for her to make her choice.

"For fuck's sake, Rebecca, bite me so we can be together!"

She moves towards him, mouth wide, and bites the air hard, taunting him. She turns her back to him and returns to her pack, the wolves howling low and long into the night.

"No! It's not fair," Daniel screams from the clearing behind. "Get back here, you bitch! It should be me! *It should be me!*"

Rebecca follows the wolf pack deep into the green, the light of the full moon finally emerging from behind the clouds, Daniel's screams fading into the wind.

RAW FOOTAGE FROM THE CUSHING'S MALL

Closed Captioning > English auto-generated. Click 🎛 *for settings.*

[CLICK OF CAMERA TURNING ON]
[CLINKING OF A METAL FENCE]
 [HEAVY BREATHING]
[LOUD CLANG OF METAL SPRINGING BACK INTO PLACE]

TOM: **** that fence is heavy.

ZAYLEE: Or maybe you're just really weak.

[GIRLS LAUGHING]

TOM: Oh yeah? Maybe I should let you hold it open on the way out.

ZAYLEE: **** that.

DANI: Don't worry, babe. I don't think any less of your biceps.

[LAUGHTER]

TOM: Thank God. Here I was, all stressed, thinking you were going to break up with me over my muscles.

DANI: And lack thereof.

TOM: Ouch. Uncalled for.

[LAUGHTER]
[GRAVEL CRUNCHING UNDERFOOT]
[RUSTLING OF LEAVES]
[TWIGS SNAPPING UNDERFOOT]

ZAYLEE: I think this would be a good spot for the intro.

DANI: You don't think it's too far back?

ZAYLEE: Maybe a bit? But it gets most of the mall in the shot with us.

DANI: I guess, but it's a little... I don't know—dull?—from so far away. Like, you can't see how gross the building is from this distance. And if it's not going to be scary then like, what's the point? You know?

ZAYLEE: Tom, what do you think?

TOM: I think it looks fine. You don't get all the details from this distance, but it's the middle of the night so... It's not like we were going to get them at this hour anyway, even with night vision on.

DANI: Yeah. I guess.

ZAYLEE: Great, so we'll do it here. Tom, you might need to

move back just a bit. Dani, maybe stand here on my left?

[FOOTSTEPS ON GRAVEL]
[CRUNCH OF DEAD LEAVES]

ZAYLEE: No, more like this.

[MOVEMENT]

DANI: Better?

ZAYLEE: Yeah, perfect.

TOM: I'm ready when you are.

ZAYLEE: You can hit record.

TOM: I did a while ago.

ZAYLEE: Why?

TOM: To get some B-roll of us coming up to the mall. I thought it looked spooky from behind the chain-link fence. It could make a good thumbnail or promo gif.

DANI: Smart.

TOM: I know.

ZAYLEE: Ready?

DANI: Yeah, sorry.

TOM: Okay. On three, two…

ZAYLEE: Whaddup guys! I'm Zaylee!

DANI: And I'm Dani! And a huge welcome back to- Can we do that again? Sorry, I just wasn't feeling it.

ZAYLEE: Yeah, I ****** up too.

[GIRLS LAUGHING]

TOM: And three, two…

ZAYLEE: Hey guys, I'm Zaylee!

DANI: And I'm Dani! Welcome back to-

ZAYLEE AND DANI: Urban Distress!

DANI: Today we're going to be checking out a relic built in the '80s that started dying slowly in the early 2000's and was finally put out of its misery in 2009 after a grease fire broke out in the food court.

ZAYLEE: That's right, folks! Today Dani, myself, and our cameraman, Tom-

DANI: Say hi, Tom!

TOM: Hi, Tom!

ZAYLEE: -will be checking out Cornwall's own abandoned Cushing's Mall.

DANI: Oooh!

ZAYLEE: While the mall has been shut down for the last seven years, there have still been reports of strange activity and even deaths happening on the property.

DANI: That's right! According to the *Cornwall Times*, a group

of students from the local high school swear they saw people walking around inside the mall a year after it closed down. However, when police came to investigate the property, the mall was empty and showed no signs of recent inhabitants.

ZAYLEE: And then, in 2011, a woman was reportedly heard screaming for help inside the building, but by the time cops arrived on the scene, she was nowhere to be found. Similar reports were made again in November of 2011, and then four more in 2012. A few months later, the body of a John Doe was allegedly found by a commercial developer who'd been interested in purchasing the property.

DANI: I'm guessing they didn't buy the dead mall.

ZAYLEE: They definitely didn't. Two more bodies, both Jane Does, were found in 2013 and 2014. Following the discovery of the last body, the city decided to put up a fence in the hopes of keeping people out.

DANI: Yeah, I'm going to go on a limb and say their plan had some *holes* in it. Get it?

ZAYLEE: Laaaaaame.

TOM: Booooo.

[DANI LAUGHING]

DANI: Well, *I* thought it was funny.

ZAYLEE: Since the fence went up, there have been fewer confirmed break-ins, but allegedly there's been an increase in strange activity.

DANI: It's true! People who live near the building, as well as joggers who pass by the mall on their morning runs, claim they've continued to hear weird noises and see shadowy figures walking around.

ZAYLEE: So tonight, we're going to take you through this relic of '80s consumerism and, hopefully, get to the bottom of the strange occurrences at the Cushing's Mall... So, how was it? Another take?

TOM: No, it was great!

ZAYLEE: Yeah?

TOM: Yeah, it was fine.

ZAYLEE: Fine or great?

TOM: It was great. You were great.

[DANI CLEARING HER THROAT]

TOM: You were great too, obviously.

DANI: Mhmm.

ZAYLEE: Are you sure? I just- I don't know. I kinda thought it was a bit stiff with Dani. No offence!

DANI: I actually felt really good about the take.

ZAYLEE: Tom, didn't you think it was a little stiff?

TOM: I mean, I don't know. Maybe a little?

DANI: Oh.

TOM: But like, it's also just the intro and I think they're always a little awkward for everyone because they're scripted.

DANI: Yeah, I guess.

ZAYLEE: Did you think I was awkward?

TOM: Well, uh-

DANI: We can do another take if you want.

ZAYLEE: No, I guess it'll be fine. I know how you are with scripted stuff. I think I was just being paranoid for nothing. You know how I am thanks to my parents. It's fine!

TOM: Yeah, I mean, everyone's better and more natural when they improvise. But, like, it was still really good!

[TOM SIGHS]

TOM: I didn't mean-

DANI: It's fine.

[FOOTSTEPS ON GRAVEL]

DANI: We should get going, otherwise we're going to be here all night.

TOM: Right.

[FOOTSTEPS ON GRAVEL]
[CRUNCH OF DEAD LEAVES]
[FOOTSTEPS ON PAVEMENT]
[ROCK SKIPPING ACROSS ASPHALT]

TOM: That one got some distance.

[ROCK SKIPPING ACROSS ASPHALT]

[GLASS SHATTERING]

DANI: Tom!

TOM: Sorry!

ZAYLEE: It's not like anyone's going to care, Dani.

DANI: I care! I don't want to cut myself on broken glass because someone thought it would be fun to kick a rock through a window. The last thing I ******* need is tetanus.

ZAYLEE: I think you only get tetanus from needles. And if your biggest concern with this place is some broken glass, boy, do I have some bad news for you.

[TOM LAUGHING]

TOM: Yeah, I'm thinking your biggest worry should be the rats or any unhoused people we accidentally surprise.

ZAYLEE: You're acting like you've never done this before.

[TONGUE CLICK]

DANI: I'm not. I just don't see the point in adding extra danger to an already dangerous situation.

ZAYLEE: You're in ******* work boots. You'll be fine.

[CLICK]

TOM: Christ, that's bright.

DANI: Oh yeah. I almost forgot.

[CLICK]

ZAYLEE: How do they look on camera?

TOM: Hold on, let me switch to night vision.

[CAMERA BEEPING]

TOM: Good.

[DOOR CREAKING OPEN]
[FOOTSTEPS ON METAL GRATE]
[DOOR SLAMS CLOSED]
[DOOR OPENING]
[FOOTSTEPS ON TILE]
[MICE SQUEAKING]

DANI: Well, at least they're not rats.

ZAYLEE: No, those are waiting for us at the back of the mall.

[LAUGHTER THAT ECHOES]

TOM: This place isn't as bad as I thought it would be.

DANI: It's probably worse in the food court.

TOM: You think?

DANI: If that's where the firefighters had to put out the grease fire, then most of the mould and water damage would be there.

TOM: True.

DANI: I'm also betting that's where any rotting will be taking place. We'll have to be extra careful where we step so we don't go through the floor.

ZAYLEE: Dibs not checking out that place first.

DANI: We should check it out together.

[FOOTSTEPS ON TILE]
[CRUNCHING OF GARBAGE UNDERFOOT]

ZAYLEE: Ooooh, Tom, get a shot of the floor there.

DANI: That's some intricate looking graffiti.

ZAYLEE: Taggers are getting weirder and weirder with their marks. Like, why do they need to draw a giant ******* circle and jam as many weird symbols into it as possible? Can't they just write their name and doodle a **** on the wall?

DANI: I think they *did* write their name in it, it just looks messy from all the paint. Lial? I think? Or maybe that's Billy? I don't know.

ZAYLEE: Well, I hope they enjoy the free publicity when people watch our ****.

[TOM LAUGHING]

DANI: *If* they watch our ****.

ZAYLEE: They will. My mom's been plugging our channel on social media whenever she can, and she told me she's trying to get the station to do a short feature about us on the evening news. Something about the feminism of urban exploration.

DANI: Oh, that would be really cool.

ZAYLEE: I guess. It's a bit boring to me, but like, I get why it might be exciting for everyone else.

DANI: You mean for people who didn't grow up with their mom's face on the side of a bus?

[ZAYLEE LAUGHING]

ZAYLEE: Yeah, exactly... Alright, I'll go scout out the shops at the end of the hall. You and Tom take these ones, and then we'll meet in the middle and figure out if anything's worth recording?

TOM: Cool.

[FOOTSTEPS ON TILE, RECEDING]
[MOVEMENT]
[ROLLING GATE LIFTS]
[FOOTSTEPS ON LINOLEUM FLOOR]
[CRUNCHING OF BROKEN GLASS]

TOM: See? Safe as can be in your work boots.

[FOOTSTEPS ON LINOLEUM FLOOR]

TOM: Oh, come on. I'm just teasing you because of earlier when-

DANI: Why do you always have to take her side?

TOM: I don't.

DANI: You do. Always. And it really sucks.

TOM: I'm sorry if you think that's what I'm doing-

[DANI SNORTING]

TOM: -but I'm just trying to be objective.

DANI: Sure.

TOM: Is this because I said you were a little stiff in the intro take? Because you've been kinda ****** since then.

DANI: I've been *what*?

TOM: You've been kinda ****** since then. Since the shoot.

DANI: Yeah, because I felt really good about how it went and then the two of you **** all over it. You could have been nice about it, but instead you took her side and made it seem like I was trash. You know how much this channel means to me. You know how important it is to my future and then you pull **** like this-

TOM: I wasn't siding with her! I was *agreeing* with her because she was right! And—I'm sorry to say this—she happens to know more than you when it comes to filming things!

DANI: Having famous parents doesn't make her innately better at recording things!

TOM: Her dad's a ******* director and her mom's a news anchor! You don't think Zaylee's picked anything up from them?

DANI: I'm just saying that-

TOM: You're just jealous, Dani. And you're taking it out on me.

DANI: I'm not!

TOM: You are!

DANI: You know, I see the way you look at her-

TOM: Oh my God, are we really doing this again?

DANI: Just admit it! Just admit you like her.

[MOVEMENT]
[PLASTIC RUBBING AGAINST FABRIC]

DANI: No, I don't want the camera. You should-

[MOVEMENT]
[PLASTIC KNOCKING AGAINST METAL JEWELRY]
[RUSTLING]

TOM: Just ******* take it.

[MICROPHONE POPS]
[FOOTSTEPS ON LINOLEUM]

TOM: I'm not doing this with you again. Find us when you're done looking around.

DANI: Tom, I'm sorry.

[FOOTSTEPS FADING]

DANI: Tom! Come back! I said I was sorry!

[FOOTSTEPS ON LINOLEUM]
[SNIFFLING]
[CRUNCHING OF PAPER UNDERFOOT]
[DANI SNEEZES]
[LONG SIGH]
[FOOTSTEPS ON LINOLEUM]
[FOOTSTEPS ON TILE]
[MICE SQUEAKING]

[MOVEMENT ABOVE]
[ROCK FALLING DOWN ESCALATOR]

DANI: Tom?

[UNINTELLIGIBLE VOICE IN THE DISTANCE]

DANI: Zaylee?

[FOOTSTEPS OVERHEAD, FADING]
[FOOTSTEPS ON METAL ESCALATOR]
[FOOTSTEPS ON TILE]

DANI: Tom, is that you?

TOM: Why can't you just leave me alone?

DANI: I just wanted to apologize.

TOM: I don't want to hear it.

DANI: Look, I know I've been acting a little crazy lately and-

TOM: I don't want you here. I don't want you at all. Nobody does... Don't you get that, Daniella? Nobody wants you.

DANI: Tom, I-

TOM: You're nothing.

DANI: Why are you being so cruel?

TOM: You keep saying you want to leave this ****hole town, but why? It was made for people like you.

DANI: Stop it! Why are you-

TOM: People who don't matter-

DANI: Tom, stop it!

TOM: -who get left behind, who get forgotten.

[FOOTSTEPS ON TILE, MOVING FAST]
[TOM'S VOICE FADES]
[SNIFFLING]
[HEAVY DOOR SWINGING OPEN]
[FOOTSTEPS ON CERAMIC TILE]
[SLAM OF DOOR CLOSING]
[THUD]
[SHAKY INHALATION]
[LONG EXHALATION]
[SNIFFLING]
[BREATHING]
[UNINTELLIGIBLE VOICES IN THE DISTANCE]
[FOOTSTEPS APPROACHING]

TOM: Dani?

[HEAVY DOOR SWINGING OPEN]
[FOOTSTEPS ON CERAMIC TILE]

TOM: Dani?

DANI: What? What do *you* want?

TOM: Where the hell have you been? Zaylee and I have been waiting for you for like ten minutes. You were supposed to be checking out your end of the mall, why the **** are you up here?

[SLAM OF DOOR CLOSING]

DANI: Are you serious right now?

TOM: We're losing shooting time. Are you coming, or what?

DANI: You want me to just film after the **** you just said to me?

TOM: Jesus Christ, Dani, still? Get over it. Zaylee was right about the shot. End of discussion. Now, are you going to finish this episode or should we just do it without you?

[DANI LAUGHING]

DANI: Unbelievable.

[FOOTSTEPS ON CERAMIC TILE]
[HEAVY DOOR SWINGING OPEN]
[FOOTSTEPS ON TILE]
[SLAM OF DOOR CLOSING]
[FOOTSTEPS ON METAL ESCALATOR]
[FOOTSTEPS ON TILE]
[MOVEMENT]

TOM: Zaylee?

ZAYLEE: Over here!

[FOOTSTEPS ON TILE]

ZAYLEE: Where have you been?

TOM: She was upstairs.

ZAYLEE: I thought we were going to check that shit out later.

TOM: Yeah, well, it seems Dani got impatient.

DANI: Are you really giving me **** after all the mean things you said about me?

ZAYLEE: Ew. You guys are fighting *again*?

DANI: It's not your business, Zay.

ZAYLEE: It is if it's going to screw up the footage for my channel.

DANI: *Our* channel.

ZAYLEE: That's what I said.

DANI: Whatever.

ZAYLEE: Anyways, I was thinking we could maybe get a shot of this store. Tom, you could take the camera into the dressing room, pan around to look at all the abandoned clothes they've left behind, and then finish up by zooming in on one of the crusty mannequins.

TOM: Love it. Dani, pass me the camera.

[MOVEMENT]
[CRUNCHING OF BROKEN GLASS]
[FOOTSTEPS, DISTANT]

DANI: What the hell was that?

TOM: What the hell was what?

[FOOTSTEPS, RECEDING]
[UNINTELLIGIBLE VOICE]

DANI: That. Didn't you hear that?

ZAYLEE: It's probably just a raccoon or something.

TOM: Yeah.

DANI: A raccoon that can talk?

[MOVEMENT]
[ROCK SKIPPING ACROSS TILE]
[FOOTSTEPS ON METAL ESCALATOR]

ZAYLEE: Oh shit. What the hell is that?

DANI: See?

ZAYLEE: So freaky.

DANI: Tom, can you check it out?

TOM: What? No. **** that noise.

ZAYLEE: Tom, go check it out.

TOM: Uh-

ZAYLEE: For me? Please?

[SIGHS]

TOM: Fine.

[FOOTSTEPS ON TILE]

DANI: For you, eh?

ZAYLEE: It's just an expression.

DANI: Not so much.

ZAYLEE: Okay, well, I didn't mean anything by it so there's no need to get your **** in a knot.

DANI: Just admit you're ******* him.

[ZAYLEE COUGHS]

ZAYLEE: Excuse me?

DANI: Just admit you're sleeping with Tom. I see the way you look at him, flirt with him. I'm not a ******* idiot, Zaylee. And even if you're *not* hitting on him, it doesn't take a genius to see that he cares about you.

ZAYLEE: Because we're friends.

DANI: We both know it's more than that.

[FOOTSTEPS ON TILE, APPROACHING]

ZAYLEE: It's not.

DANI: Oh my God, Dani! Just admit it! We've been friends since we were kids, you don't think I can tell when you're ******* lying? Just grow some balls, and admit it!

ZAYLEE: There's nothing to admit!

DANI: You're a ******* liar, Zaylee!

TOM: Is everything okay?

DANI: Obviously not!

TOM: What's going o-

ZAYLEE: Did you see anything?

TOM: No, nothing.

DANI: Good, because I need some air.

[FOOTSTEPS ON TILE, MOVING FAST]

TOM: What the hell is wrong with her tonight?

ZAYLEE: I don't know. Maybe the pressure of everything is getting to her…

[TOM AND ZAYLEE'S VOICES FADE]
[HEAVY BREATHING]
[SNIFFLING]
[MEASURED BREATHING]
[FOOTSTEPS ON TILE, APPROACHING]

DANI: What do you want?

ZAYLEE: What do I want? For you to go away. For you to leave, Daniella.

DANI: *You* followed *me* over here. What are you-

ZAYLEE: He doesn't love you. You know that, right?

DANI: Excuse me?

ZAYLEE: Tom doesn't love you. I don't love you. Nobody does.

DANI: Stop it. What are you-

ZAYLEE: You're worthless, Daniella. You always will be. Do you know why I work with you?

DANI: Because we've been friends since-

ZAYLEE: So people will like me more; charity work gets views. And, I mean, that's all you are, right? A charity case. Like everyone else in this small, dirty, town.

DANI: Why are-

ZAYLEE: When people watch our videos, they're not going to see you. They're going to see me. Just me. Everyone in town already knows who I am. That I'm someone who's going places. That I'm going to outshine my ******* family. But you?

DANI: Get away from me!

[FOOTSTEPS ON TILE, MOVING FAST]

ZAYLEE: You're no one, Daniella. And you're never leaving.

[ZAYLEE'S VOICE FADES]
[HEAVY BREATHING]
[SNIFFLING]
[HICCUPS]
[FOOTSTEPS ON TILE, SLOWING DOWN]

DANI: Zaylee? How are you already back from the atrium? I thought I-

[FOOTSTEPS ON TILE, STOPPING ABRUPTLY]
[SMACKING OF LIPS]
[PANTING]
[GASP]
[MOMENTARY SILENCE]

TOM: Dani, it's not what it looks like.

ZAYLEE: It's not what you think.

DANI: I knew it!

[SOBBING]

DANI: I ******* knew it!

TOM: Dani, please-

DANI: This whole time! *This whole ******* time*!

TOM: Dani, just listen to me-

DANI: And you kept telling me I was ******* crazy! How could you?

TOM: Please, Dani, it doesn't mean anything.

ZAYLEE: What?

TOM: Babe, I'm sorry.

DANI: Leave me alone!

[FOOTSTEPS ON TILE, MOVING FAST]
[SOBS]
[HEAVY BREATHING]
[FOOTSTEPS ON METAL ESCALATOR]
[FOOTSTEPS ON TILE, MOVING FAST]
[FLOOR GROANING]
[SHAKY BREATHING]

TOM: How did you think this was going to end, Daniella?

DANI: How did you get here so-

TOM: Did you really think you were important to me?

DANI: Stop saying this!

[UNINTELLIGIBLE VOICE IN THE DISTANCE]

TOM: To Zaylee?

[FOOTSTEPS ON TILE, APPROACHING]
[TOM'S VOICE IN THE DISTANCE]

TOM: Dani? Where are you?

[FLOOR GROANING]
[MOVEMENT]

TOM: You're nothing, Daniella.

DANI: Please, *please*, just leave me alone.

[TOM'S VOICE IN THE DISTANCE]

TOM: Dani, are you in the food court?

[BREATHING GETTING LOUDER]

TOM: Did you really think you could leave here, Daniella? You?

[FOOTSTEPS APPROACHING]
[FLOOR GROANING]

TOM: Dani, please, I'm sorry.

TOM: You're not going anywhere.

TOM: Dani, come this way.

DANI: Leave me alone!

TOM: You're nothing.

TOM: The floor's unsafe, you said so yourself. It's warping underneath you and I'm worried it's going to give out. Please, *please*, move towards me. Slowly.

DANI: I said go away!

TOM: And you'll always be nothing.

[FOOTSTEPS APPROACHING, SLOWLY]
[FLOOR GROANS]
[WOOD CREAKING]

TOM: Dani, please, take my hand.

DANI: I said go away!

[MOVEMENT]
[THUMP OF HANDS COLLIDING WITH SOMETHING SOLID]
[TOM GRUNTS]
[WOOD CRACKS]
[FLOOR GROANS]
[SCREAM]
[THUD]
[WOOD CRASHING ONTO TILE]
[GASPING]
[HEAVY BREATHING]

DANI: Oh my God. Tom. Tom!

[FOOTSTEPS ON TILE, MOVING FAST]
[FOOTSTEPS ON METAL ESCALATOR]

[CRASH OF THE PLASTIC CAMERA ON TILE]
[GLASS CRACKING]
[THUMP OF DANI'S KNEES ON TILE]

DANI: Oh God. Oh God, Tom, I'm so sorry. I didn't mean to-
I'm so sorry.

[CHOKING]
[LABOURED BREATHING]
[SUDDEN SILENCE]
[DANI WAILS]

ZAYLEE: You killed him.

DANI: No!

ZAYLEE: You murdered him.

DANI: I didn't! I didn't mean to. He wouldn't go away so-

ZAYLEE: Everyone's going to know it's your fault.

[UNINTELLIGIBLE VOICE IN THE DISTANCE]

DANI: -I just pushed him. I didn't mean for the floor-

ZAYLEE: You couldn't stand him being with me.

DANI: -to just give out.

[SOBS]

ZAYLEE: So you killed him.

DANI: I didn't mean to.

[FOOTSTEPS ON TILE, APPROACHING]

[ZAYLEE'S VOICE IN THE DISTANCE]

ZAYLEE: Tom? Dani? Where the **** are you guys?

ZAYLEE: They're all going to know, Daniella. Everyone. They're going to see what you did. They're going to see what Tom and I already knew. That you're worthless.

[FOOTSTEPS ON TILE, APPROACHING]

ZAYLEE: Dani? Jesus, there you are-

[SCREAM]

ZAYLEE: Oh my God! Tom! Dani, what happened?

[FOOTSTEPS ON TILE, MOVING FAST]

ZAYLEE: Go on, Daniella. Admit it. You killed him.

DANI: I didn't!

ZAYLEE: You didn't *what*? Dani, what the **** happened?

[MOVEMENT]

ZAYLEE: I don't think he's breathing!

ZAYLEE: Go on, Daniella. Admit it. ******* admit it!

DANI: No!

ZAYLEE: Call 9-1-1!

ZAYLEE: Tell me you killed him!

DANI: No! I didn't!

ZAYLE: What?!

ZAYLEE: Tell me you did it!

DANI: No!

[MOVEMENT]
[CHEST COMPRESSIONS]
[CRYING]

ZAYLEE: Tom, wake up.

ZAYLEE: But he won't wake up, will he, Daniella?

[SOBBING]

ZAYLEE: Please wake up.

ZAYLEE: Have you always been jealous of me?

ZAYLEE: Tom, oh God. Tom.

ZAYLEE: What do you think people will say about me when they find out I heroically tried to stop you from killing your boyfriend?

DANI: That's not what happened!

ZAYLEE: What? What the **** are you saying?!

ZAYLEE: That's what I'll tell them.

DANI: You wouldn't ******* dare.

ZAYLEE: Dani, you're scaring me!

ZAYLEE: Daniella was crazy. A woman possessed.

ZAYLEE: Dani? Dani?!

ZAYLEE: I'll be on every show. You'll see me everywhere, Daniella.

ZAYLEE: Dani, what did you do?

[MOVEMENT]
[HEAVY BREATHING]

DANI: I'll ******* kill you!

ZAYLEE: Wha-

[THUD OF PEOPLE FALLING INTO EACH OTHER]
[SHOUTING]
[SHOUTS STOP]
[CHOKING]
[WHEEZING]
[NAILS SCRATCHING SKIN]
[DANI'S PAINED SHOUTS]
[OPEN-PALM SLAPS]
[GASPS FOR BREATH]
[GURGLING]
[SUDDEN SILENCE]
[THUMP OF BODY HITTING TILE]
[HEAVY BREATHING]
[FOOTSTEPS ON TILE, RECEDING]
[UNINTELLIGIBLE VOICES IN THE DISTANCE]
[CLICK OF CAMERA SHUTTING OFF]

SPLINTER

Leila stands beside the shrub and points to it, looking like a Vanna White in tan overalls. She continues to smile and gesture at the underwhelming bush before frowning and crossing her arms over her chest.

"You hate it."

It's not a question.

"I don't *hate* it. I just don't get why you like it."

"What's not to like?"

"Well, it just… You don't find it looks like that shitty tree they decorate in *A Charlie Brown Christmas*?"

"What? No! I mean, okay, it could use some love, but it's not *that* bad," Leila argues.

Malorie gives the plant a once-over, trying to be as uncritical as she can. The shrub is small and bare, with rough branches peeking through the gaps where the leaves have either wilted or fallen off completely. What foliage does remain isn't half as bright or half as green as the image on the sticker that had been slapped on its plastic pot. Even the bright red fruit that gives the Canada buffaloberry bush its name is few and far between on the small plant.

"It looks like garbage the city forgot to pick up, Leila," Malorie says honestly. "I doubt this thing will survive until Friday, let alone through the summer, and even with the 30%-off tag it's pretty expensive."

"It's not *that* expensive."

Malorie grabs a branch of the tree and bends it between her fingers, frowning to herself when it snaps right off the bush. She grabs another one and tests it too, breaking the limb off the small plant.

"Stop doing that, you're hurting it," Leila chastises.

"Hurting it? The thing is already dead. I bet the berries

aren't even sweet."

She carelessly grabs a small handful of berries from the shrub, tearing off some of the fragile leaves along with the bright red fruit, and pops one into her mouth, grimacing as the bitter juice coats her tongue. She throws the rest of the berries onto the ground beside the potted bush and spits out the masticated fruit.

"Disgusting," Malorie says.

"In fairness, I think you're supposed to boil them with sugar before you eat them," Leila says defensively. "And if it's bearing fruit, it's obviously not dead; you're just being mean."

"I'm not being mean, I'm being realistic. We came here to get plants for the back garden and now that we have more than a shaded balcony, I don't think this mess is worth bringing home. Our bill is going to be big enough as it is."

Leila frowns and nods in agreement. "Yeah, I guess," she says, running a hand gently over the leaves of the buffaloberry bush and trying to arrange them to cover the bald spot caused by Malorie's carelessness. She wistfully strokes the leaves, tilting her head and admiring the almost-barren plant. It's pathetic and pulls on Malorie's heartstrings, just like Leila knows it will. Eventually, she gets up from the shrub with a forlorn sigh, and Malorie can't help but give in.

"Ugh, fine, we can get it. But that's the only decrepit bush we buy today! The rest of the garden needs to survive until the fall."

"Deal!" Leila shouts, excited. She crosses the distance between herself and the flatbed cart filled to the brim with flowers and tries to rearrange the plants to make space for the dying bush. It's clear within a few minutes that even with the bush's unnaturally small stature, there isn't enough room on the wooden dolly for the plant to fit.

"Do you want me to just carry it?" Malorie asks.

"I don't want you getting your shirt dirty," Leila says, motioning to the dry earth stuck to the side of the planter.

"Yeah, it would be a real shame if the shirt I use exclusively for manual labour and dirty jobs was to get a speck of dirt on it. How would I ever survive?"

"Ha. Ha," Leila says. She gets up from her spot next to the cart, making sure the flowers have all been put back on it, and begins to push it down the nursery lane. "I'll meet you at the cash," she says, blowing a kiss to the other woman as she navigates through the rows of plants and Saturday-morning shoppers.

Malorie sighs at the sad-looking shrub, unable to see the beauty in it, before bending down and grabbing the plastic pot.

"Ow!" she shouts, letting go of the Canada buffaloberry and shaking her hand in the air. She looks at the web of skin between her index finger and thumb, hissing under her breath as she examines the splinter that's made its way under her skin. The tiny sliver of wood—which looks almost black buried in her hand—is too deep for her to pull out with her short nails and too painful for her to ignore. She grumbles to herself before bending back down, making sure the plastic is now free of splinters, and she picks the shrub up with one arm before following Leila to the register.

"Are you sure you don't want help unloading the car? I really don't mind," Leila says disingenuously, her hand already wrapped around the door handle of the small hatchback. She looks at her parents' house from the window, smiling as she spots the tiny Yorkie jumping and hollering from behind their screen door.

"Nah, I'll be fine. Besides, if it gets me out of an afternoon with the in-laws, I'll happily do it myself."

Leila laughs, lightly slapping Malorie's arm. "Hey, you love my family!"

"I do, but don't tell them that. Otherwise, how will I get out of barbecues and family events I'm not in the mood to go to?" Malorie asks, eyes wide in mock distress. "Did you need me to come and pick you up later tonight or—"

"No no, I'm sure one of them will drive me over after supper. If they break out the wine, *then* I might give you a call."

"Duly noted," she says, leaning over and kissing Leila goodbye. "Have a fun time tonight!"

Leila opens the door and hops out of the car, waving to Malorie. "You too!"

Malorie waits until her partner is inside the house before taking off down the road, absentmindedly rubbing her sore and itchy hand against her jeans as she drives. The splinter is deep enough that it doesn't catch on her pants, but sore enough that the friction is uncomfortable. The light ahead of her turns red and she slows to a stop, taking a minute to look at her palm.

Her skin is bright red and inflamed, veins of black spreading out from around the puckered puncture site. Her hand throbs in time with her heartbeat and radiates warmth. She flexes her thumb and index finger, bending them one at a time and then together, and she finds the movement difficult for her now-stiff hand. The lights go from red to green and back to red as she examines her hand, thankful that the road behind her is empty. This time, when the lights blink back to green, she peels down the quiet road and rushes home.

The bathroom light is stronger than she remembers and it burns her eyes as she tries to focus on her hand. Sweat rolls down her face and she wipes her forehead with the back of her arm. When did her house get so stuffy? She pushes the tweezers against her skin, pinches the wood between the metal legs, and pulls. She sighs with relief as the dark shard slips out from inside her hand and then grumbles when she realizes a sliver of it is still embedded in her flesh. She keeps fiddling with the tweezers, pressing them harder and harder into her soft skin, but eventually gives up when she realizes she's just pushing the splinter deeper. She washes her hand with soap and cool water, pours a generous helping of hydrogen peroxide on the tender skin, and then applies some antibiotic cream and a bandage to the wound. Her hand is still sore, but she's hopeful it will get better now that the majority of the wood has been removed.

Determined to at least get some of the planting done before Leila comes home, Malorie heads back out to the car—mentally noting to also sweep up the dirt she tracked in before her wife sees it—and begins unloading the flowers. She carries the styrofoam flats through the small wooden fence into the backyard, hand throbbing, and places them on the grass beside the pine deck. The normally sweet smell of the wood is suddenly overwhelming and it makes her head swim and her stomach heave. She moves away from the pine, body stiff and sore, and heads back to the car for the next set of flowerbeds.

She leans into the trunk and slides two more flats of annuals towards her, squinting at how bright the plants look, and how visible her veins are, in the afternoon sun. Their leaves shine neon green and their petals are blindingly bright. Her head feels heavy and her thoughts are thick like sap, and she struggles to remember what she came out to the car for. The perfume of the flowers burns her nose and stings the back of her throat, the pain reminding her of the task at hand. She carries the flowers through the yard and places them with the others, trying to move away from the sickening pine as fast as her stiff legs will take her. She repeats the process twice more, the web of injured skin on her hand complaining the whole time, before finally heading back to retrieve the Canada buffaloberry bush.

The shrub looks different to her in the harsh glow of the sun. Its leaves are too green and its berries are too red, and even the black plastic of its planter looks too dark to be real, like the bush is growing out of an empty void. Even her skin looks wrong in the light, sickly pale and tinged chartreuse. She closes her eyes, head swimming, and breathes in through her nose and out through her mouth, trying to calm her body down. It feels like her skin is vibrating on her bones, pulsating with discomfort, and the cool air on her flesh is refreshing. She inhales, her body expanding with her lungs as it drinks in the refreshing oxygen, and exhales with a sigh. She picks the plant up, closes the trunk, and brings it into the backyard, leaving the gate open behind her.

The branches of the buffaloberry scratch her arm, the rough wood ripping at tender flesh that feels paper-thin to her, as she carries it over the grass and towards the flowers. The smell of the pine deck grows stronger with each step she takes in its direction, and Malorie decides to plant the bush near the gateway instead. She tells herself it's so the plant will already be close to the trash bins when it eventually dies, but she knows it's to avoid the stench of the wood and the burning colours of the flower petals.

She leaves the bush on the grass and moves to the small shed in the corner of the yard, her joints aching with each step. Her body feels tight and sore, and her hand is throbbing in time with her heartbeat. She flicks the light on and looks around the space, tucking the small garden trowel into her back pocket along with a pair of work gloves. She goes to flick the light off but struggles to bend her fingers, eventually pushing the button down with her forearm. She holds her arm up to the sun, throat tightening as she sees her hand.

Her skin is rough and ashen brown, thick bark now coating the area that used to be flesh. Her fingers are bent and immobile, bone and sinew replaced with solid wood to her elbow. Above the joint, her arm is bright green with veins of emerald that wrap their way up to her shoulder and creep beneath the collar of her sleeveless tee. She frantically lifts her shirt with one hand to see that her abdomen is a swirling mess of flesh and flora. The bandage on her hand bulges out, something pressing against the fabric, and she rips it off. The small puncture wound is now wide and gaping. The tip of a small branch juts out of where the splinter once was, bright red berries visible beneath the surface. Malorie tries to scream but finds her throat tight and silent.

She stumbles through the yard, struggling to move her rigid legs trapped under solid skin. She trips over herself and falls to the grass, her chest growing heavy and beginning to swell as something moves and expands inside. She tries to scream again, this time for help, but instead, she chokes as bright red berries tumble through her open lips and spill onto the ground around her.

Leila waves to her dad from the driveway, watching him drive down the small road and out of sight, the amber sunset blinding her as it slowly fades and darkens to indigo. She stares after his car for a long while, stomach full with good food and great drinks, before turning back to her house. She starts walking down the front path before noticing the back gate propped open.

"Malorie?" she calls out, heading towards the backyard instead.

Leila pulls the gate open and peeks in. She spots the flowerbeds against the deck and the small bush discarded on the grass nearby and is about to get annoyed with Malorie's carelessness until she sees the plant in the middle of the yard. It's another buffaloberry shrub, only this one is massive. Its leaves are parakeet green and stretch up into the sky, making the plant look more like a tree than a bush. On its sturdy brown branches hang bushels of candy-red fruit, glistening like rubies in the light. Leila crosses the space to the bush, closing the gate behind her with a soft click, unable to stop herself from plucking a handful of the berries and popping them into her mouth. They're juicy and sweet, and she runs her hand across her mouth as some of the red trails down her chin. She eats another handful, savouring the taste as the fruit explodes across her tongue, before noticing the discarded trowel and gloves on the grass nearby.

She shakes her head at the mess and climbs the stairs of the deck, opening the back door of the small house as she calls out to Malorie.

STICKY SWEET

Sticky sweet, like honey,
the scent floods her senses
and drowns her in waves
of candied figs and syrup.
It pulls her through the woods,
off her path home and away from safety,
deep into the blackened heart of the forest.
The tree stands proud,
branches reaching to the sky, wrapped in green,
trunk black like tar, like molasses, like burnt sugar.
The air is thick with the warm smell.
It washes over her, coats her tongue,
and drips down her throat.
It pulls her close, drawing her in,
working its magic from deep in her lungs.
She moves closer, letting the sweetness guide her.
The trunk moves, shimmers,
ripples in the blackness
that mesmerize and terrify.
She touches the bark,
the rough tree soft beneath her fingers.
She steps closer, fingers numb,
and wraps her arms around the green spire,
resting her face on the trunk
that should scratch and chafe,
but molds and softens to the curves of her body.
She breathes deep the sweetness,
body blind to the nectar turned acid.
She shifts in discomfort, skin prickling at the slow burn,
but is glued to the tree, skin melting to sap.
She opens an eye, that waters from the fumes,

and she watches her hand, peach turning plum,
smooth skin softening, liquefying,
rolling off bone and blending with black,
as her flesh coats the trunk.
She inhales, liquid gurgling in half dissolved lungs,
enjoying the smell, sticky sweet,
of her body deliquescing
and blending with those before her
as she's devoured by the tree.

BROKEN

Once upon a time there lived the King of the East, who was never satisfied and was always left wanting. He desired to rule an empire so big he would one day be known as the King of a Thousand Kings, but the King of the West had the same ambition. Soon, the day came when both kings turned their eyes to the Middle World with longing and hunger.

The King of the West promised that he would crush his enemies with the force of a thousand lions. The King of the East promised to undo his foes with the wisdom of a thousand clever serpents. And so both kingdoms raged war with the other for the Middle World. Though the West was fierce in battle, they could not outsmart the East. Although the East was wise, they did not possess the strength to match the West in combat.

Neither could win.

For a thousand years the kingdoms fought until, one day, there was a King of the West and a King of the East who were born content. They grew up to be loving and compassionate men, who wished only for their people to be happy. Both kings wanted peace, and so they signed a treaty that would unite the Western and Eastern kingdoms.

It was decided that the firstborn daughter of the Western Kingdom would marry the firstborn son of the Eastern Kingdom and together they would rule the Middle World. On the eve of the daughter's eighteenth birthday, the young man would be sent to the Western Kingdom, and the two would be wed.

The King of the East's son was born a year later. He was raised to be compassionate like his father. He was taught to show mercy and to put those he ruled before himself. The Only Son grew to be smart, strong, and—above all else—

loving.

In the Western Kingdom, the First Daughter was born two years after the Only Son. She was raised to be strong, fair, and certain in her actions. But while she was fair, she was uncaring, and though she did what was right for the many, she was not sympathetic for the few that her decisions affected. She grew up to be strong, but so did her heart.

The Second Daughter was born a year after that, and she was taught to be kind, respectful, and trusting. She treated her servants with the same respect and dignity with which she treated her friends. She grew up in privilege and, in return, did her best to help those who suffered hardships. Unlike her sister, she grew up to know love, and so did her heart.

The First Daughter's eighteenth birthday came and soon after its passing the Only Son arrived. He was greeted by the King and Queen of the West, and introduced to their daughters. He was brought to the First Daughter and though she was strong, he knew that he did not love her. He was then brought to the Second Daughter and though he knew she could not be his wife, he loved her more than anyone.

While they waited for the wedding, the Only Son took the Second Daughter into the gardens and they talked about things only the closest of friends discussed. He knew in his heart that he was meant to be with her forever. The Second Daughter was happy and though she had known love, she had never felt it so completely. It was the Only Son that her heart sang for.

But they both knew that if he did not marry her sister, there would be conflict for another thousand years. And so the two were filled with sadness at the approaching wedding.

The First Daughter, however, had never been so happy. Never had she ever seen a person that she loved as much as the Only Son. She had only known the burden of duty all her life, and was eager to share her future with someone who both loved her unconditionally and understood the responsibility that had been thrust upon her. She knew she would never love another man as much as she loved him. And so her heart beat fast in anticipation of their wedding.

At the ceremony, the Only Son said his "I do's" with a heavy heart. And though the Second Daughter looked on in apparent joy, her heart cried a thousand silent tears for the man she loved.

Days passed, and while the First Daughter was inseparable from her husband, the Only Son had eyes only for the Second Daughter. And so, when the First Daughter was asleep in their bed, he crept from their room and moved through the shadows to find the woman his heart yearned for. He opened the door to the Second Daughter's room and found her sitting at the windowsill, looking out into the night and crying softly. She had done this every day since the marriage. The Only Son urged her to get dressed and follow him to the river.

Soon, the Second Daughter was moving swiftly through the palace gardens and to the riverbank. There, she embraced him by the moonlit water. He told her what they were about to do was wrong, and that if her sister found out it would surely kill her.

"And betraying our hearts," the Second Daughter whispered, "will surely kill us."

So they held each other and made love under the stars, and were unaware that the First Daughter had awoken in the night, chilled by the wind from her open door. They were unaware that she had watched her sister follow the same footpaths her husband had taken only moments before. They were unaware that the First Daughter had pursued them to the river, had hidden behind a tree, and had caught them in the act. Betrayed, the First Daughter ran back to her room, and as the sun slowly rose overhead a rage that had previously been unknown to her grew in her heart.

The Only Son did not return to their bed in the early hours of the morning. At the dining hall, she came to discover that the Only Son and the Second Daughter were eating together at the great table after a morning walk through the gardens. The First Daughter, stung by the betrayal, lovingly asked her husband why he had not woken her to break fast with him. Unable to meet her gaze, he lied that it was because she had looked so peaceful in sleep that he couldn't bear to wake her.

The First Daughter looked at her sister and asked her if she would like to accompany her to the Northern Wood the next morning to keep her from feeling lonely while her husband was away. He was to survey the Middle World, and she dreaded to think how sad she'd be in his absence. The Second Daughter, unable to look her sister in the eyes, agreed.

The day passed and the night came, and like the one before it, the Only Son left for the river with his lover, and the First Daughter once again found herself alone in her marriage bed. Only this time, instead of counting the hours until sunup, she began to set her plan in motion, writing a letter by candlelight and hiding it in the pocket of her gown.

The sun rose and the Only Son departed on his journey, leaving behind his wife and the woman he loved.

Both sisters spent the day riding through the Northern Wood with their guards. When they returned to the fortress walls, the First Daughter asked her sister if she would accompany her to her favourite spot in all the realm: the river. The Second Daughter, ashamed of her actions, agreed. Their guards, dismissed by the Second Daughter after a day of hard work, did not follow.

Upon their arrival at the riverbank, the First Daughter pointed to something in the water and asked her sister if she knew what it was. The Second Daughter, unable to see the object clearly, wandered close to the water's edge. The First Daughter pointed down into the water. The Second Daughter, curious still, wandered out into the shallows with her sister close behind. The First Daughter, voice trembling with excitement, pointed at the blue beside her sister. The Second Daughter leaned closer to the water.

It was then that the First Daughter struck.

She pushed her sister's head under the water, holding her below the current. She thrashed and struggled, but soon her body was still and she was drowned next to the very riverbank where she and the Only Son had broken the eldest daughter's heart.

The First Daughter waded out of the water, watching as her sister was pulled out of sight by the current. After a moment of quiet celebration, she ran to the castle walls screaming for the guards. She howled in mock sorrow as she recounted her sister's misfortune. Through fake tears, she told the men how the Second Daughter had wandered away from her sister's side and thrown herself in the river. She told them she had run in after her when the poor girl hadn't resurfaced, but when the coursing water threatened to drag her under too, she'd lost her courage and pulled herself from the river to seek help. The guards rushed on horses to the riverbank in the hopes of saving the Second Daughter, who was much beloved across the Western Kingdom.

Alone, the First Daughter made her way to her room, where she lay on her bed and laughed into the pillows until her chest hurt as much as her heart had. After some time, she was quiet, and she waited in silence for the guards to bring back her sister's body. Eventually, there was a knock on her door, and her parents entered holding a letter that had been found on the Second Daughter's pillow.

It was addressed to her.

With shaking hands, the First Daughter read the letter aloud. It spoke of how the Second Daughter was unhappy. It confessed that she also loved the Only Son, but knew he was destined to be with her sister. The letter spoke of how she wanted to be his queen, and if she couldn't be that then she refused to be anyone else's. As the First Daughter read the note, no one suspected her treachery. None of them knew her hands shook from fear, worried that they might recognize the writing as her own. Or, worse, that they might confess that they had seen her slip into her sister's room and leave the letter on the bed when she thought no one was looking.

The guards returned soon after she had finished reading the letter, with her sister's body that had been dredged from the water.

The Only Son returned to the Western Kingdom, brought home by the sad news that had found him. There was a grand funeral held for the Second Daughter and mourners from all corners of the realm came to pay their respects to her. Of all those saddened by her passing, the Only Son's heart was the heaviest of them all. He blamed himself for her death and in time his heart became like stone.

He became uncaring to the people of the kingdom and even more so to the First Daughter. He stopped loving and wallowed in sadness. He shut himself away from the people he ruled and rarely did he leave the castle walls. When he did, it was only to visit the river where he would cry silently for his lover. Only then would he let himself feel and love and mourn.

But the Only Son's sadness was not felt by him alone.

The First Daughter felt his pain too, but in a way she had not expected. She had thought with the passing of her sister, her husband would cling to her for comfort and love her back as fiercely as she loved him. Instead, he withdrew into himself. He couldn't bear looking at her, the love in her eyes a reminder of the way the Second Daughter would look at him. This, above all else, cut the First Daughter to the bone. His neglect began to wear on her until she could no longer take the pain of it.

Becoming desperate, she soon convinced herself the only way to relieve his suffering was to make him fall in love with her the way he had fallen in love with the Second Daughter. And so, with the sun not yet on the horizon, she snuck into the stables and fled the castle for the Northern Wood.

She rode past the great oak trees and strong maples. She headed for the center of the forest, where she knew the witch was waiting. The First Daughter recognized the Old Woman as a witch her father had given sanctuary in the forest when villagers had wanted her dead. At the time she hadn't understood why her father had spared the elderly woman's life. But at present, she was glad her father had been kind.

The Old Woman asked the First Daughter why she had come to see her, and the young woman explained that it was so her husband could love her the way she loves him. The Old Woman looked at her with sadness and told her that even if she helped the Only Son fall in love with her, it would never be real.

"As long as I can feel loved by my husband, I'll be content."

The Old Woman told her that if she enchanted her husband, the love would feel emptier with each passing day. She told her that only his true love for the Second Daughter could break the spell, and that if he ever learned of her treachery, he would turn into a creature as monstrous and evil as her sororicide. Though frightened by the Old Woman's knowledge of her crime and what would happen if the Only Son ever discovered her transgression, she took the potion. She paid the witch a handsome fee and rode back to the castle before her husband woke.

While the Only Son broke fast, the First Daughter brought him a goblet carrying a drink laced with the potion. No other drink had been laid out for him at her behest. He nodded his thanks and brought it to his mouth. As his lips touched the cup and he swallowed its contents, her heart raced and her hands quivered. She watched, hopeful, as the Only Son's eyes came alight with a spark. He looked at the First Daughter and there was a passion in his soul that hadn't been there before.

And for the first time in a long time, she was happy.

But happiness was fleeting, and as time wore on, she became less content. Though the Only Son looked at her with love, she felt nothing. Though his words were honey-sweet, they tasted bitter. Though his hands touched her body with passion, she felt only the warmth of his body and none from his soul.

The First Daughter became desperate as she tried to love him as she once had, but like the witch had promised, she was empty. Starved, she became angry and desperate for love, *any* love. But all forms of affection grew cold and foreign to her as the months wore on.

Desperate for release from her newfound torment, the First Daughter decided to prostrate herself before her husband and ask for mercy. And she believed that maybe, just *maybe*, once she told him all she had done to be with him, the spell would break and he would realize that she had been his true love all along.

And so, one night when the moon was high in the blackened sky and they were alone in their bedroom, the First Daughter asked the Only Son if he loved her. He told her that he did. She asked him if he'd forgive her even if he didn't yet know what for. He said he would, unconditionally.

And so she told him everything.

She told the Only Son how she had caught him and her sister at the river, how her heart had broken and turned to rot in her chest. She told him how she had become rageful and bitter and had dragged her sister under the river's current. She told him how she had written a letter in her sister's hand, had tried to make him love her, and had given him a potion when all was lost.

The light in his eyes dimmed to black and, for the first time in the longest of times, she loved him.

Before she could beg him for forgiveness, the Only Son let out a guttural scream. It was full of rage, pain, and grief. His cries grew louder as he grew taller, his skin stretching away and shedding from his body as his spine elongated. His limbs fell away and his jaw cracked open wide, teeth replaced by giant fangs, as he transformed into an immense snake-like creature, towering above the First Daughter.

Never before had she been so afraid. She moved towards the door, but the monster moved too. The First Daughter ran towards the window, grasping for any possible escape, but she'd been doomed the moment she held the Second Daughter under the current of the river. The creature struck, fangs digging deep into her flesh as he pulled her chest apart and ate his fill. Satiated, he slithered out through the open door, along the hallways, and out into the courtyard, where he was spotted by the guards. They took up their weapons and struck the beast down, killing it as it made its escape for the river.

The following morning when the servants went to wake the Only Son and the First Daughter, they found their bed empty and room bloodied. The skin of the Only Son was left discarded on the floor. The First Daughter had been torn apart, her heart ripped from her chest and consumed by the creature she'd once loved.

And none of them lived happily ever after.

IN UTERO

She pushes the hook through, holding it tightly with the needle-nose pliers. The thread is uncomfortable and she grimaces as it catches on her skin. She makes a simple overhand knot, then a second and a third. She couldn't quite figure out the surgeon's knot, so she tells herself this will have to do. She cuts off the excess thread and repeats the process down the length of her abdomen, impressed with how straight she'd made the incision.

When she's finished, she pours the antiseptic over the sutures and pushes herself up out of the chair, holding onto the back of it as she rediscovers her centre of gravity.

She looks at herself in the full-length mirror, smiling as she puts a protective hand on her stomach. She feels him kick and scream, and hopes that he'll soon be quiet.

She misses being pregnant but she hates being a mom.

EVERYTHING SHE'S LOOKING FOR

"I think I want to break up with you."

"Oh my God, shut up," she laughs. "I said I was sorry."

"No, I mean it," the other woman jokes, "I think we need to break up. I was promised a night of—how did the e-vite phrase it?—'furiously feminist and devilishly divine fun.' That, Morgan, was fucking lame."

The leaves crunch underfoot as they walk through the dimly lit park, putting distance between themselves and the small university-owned townhouse a few streets over. The air is cool on their skin and promises rain. Wind rushes through the trees and rattles the branches, shaking out the last of the autumn-red foliage onto the ground ahead of them. The stars are bright overhead, or they would be if not for the glowing city lights drowning out their natural beauty.

"I didn't know you were into that Wicca shit," Ari continues with a smile.

"I'm not! Or like, not like whatever the hell that was."

"Sure, whatever you say. Next thing I know you'll be BFFs with Raven Blackfeather Ceridwen and her troupe of radical truth-seeking sisters of the moon."

Morgan laughs, nearly doubling over. "*Man*, was she pretentious or what?"

"I mean, what else were you expecting from a university Wiccan group?"

"Can you say their title properly, please? They were *very* clear about how they identified their organization," Morgan quips.

"Right, sorry. What did you expect from a university-funded interfaith coven for socially-conscious babes made of starlight?"

The two of them laugh with abandon before Morgan thinks to make sure none of the other meeting members are within earshot. Thankfully the two are alone in the park as they head to the student housing district a few blocks over. With cheap rent, cheap amenities (like the park), and cheap bars within walking distance of nearly all the downtown campus buildings, Laughlan Street East is known primarily for housing most of the city's university students. With a variety of apartment buildings practically stacked on top of each other for a three-block radius, most of the students are—to some varying degree—both neighbours and classmates. Which is no exception for Morgan and Ari, who had found themselves in the same Research Methods class and apartment complex.

"I don't know. I mean, I guess something more... *more*. Like, I guess I was expecting them to do small spells and rituals, maybe. And like, get more involved with protests and social justice work. Not sit in a living room and act pretentious while drowning in a sea of palo santo."

"Yeah, that was a lot."

"So strong," Morgan agrees. "The smell was the most powerful thing about that group."

"I'll take it you're not planning on joining them for next month's Goddess Circle?"

"I'd sooner choke," Morgan retorts.

The two of them walk in silence for a bit, the noise of the downtown core filtering through the trees. The park, although small, is like a green shelter from the all-consuming sea of grey brick around them. The maples offer shade on hot days and something sturdy to make out against at night, and even without most of their leaves, they dull the noise of drunk students and honking cars. Their building, the tallest one on the rapidly approaching block, is obscured from view thanks to a collection of lush pines in the distance.

"So, what made you want to go tonight? Spirituality?

New friends?" Ari asks in earnest.

"Oh, it doesn't matter. It's stupid."

"I doubt it. Come on, you can tell me."

Morgan exhales and looks away from her, embarrassed, though not for the first time that evening. "The magic." Ari laughs and Morgan crosses her arms in front of her chest defensively. "I told you it was stupid."

"Oh, no, sorry! I wasn't laughing at you, I promise. And that's not stupid."

"I feel pretty stupid," Morgan admits.

"No, don't! Really, don't. You're not stupid, you're wonderful." She paws at Morgan's arms, uncrossing them and taking her hands in Ari's own, pulling her closer. "I was laughing that you went to a bunch of Wiccans for a taste of magic when I'm right here."

"You are *so* lame when you're trying to be romantic," Morgan laughs, leaning in and kissing Ari on the lips. "Thankfully you're cute."

"First of all, I'm gorgeous," she teases. "And secondly, I wasn't trying to be romantic, I was being serious."

They continue through the park, out to the main street, and then cross at the intersection to their building. They open the main glass door, punch the door code onto the second one, and get in the small elevator together. The two of them get off on the sixth floor and Ari walks Morgan to her door.

"Well tonight was... interesting," Ari laughs, as Morgan unlocks her apartment.

"You could say that."

Ari chuckles and leans in, planting a soft kiss on Morgan's cheek. "Have I mentioned how beautiful you look tonight? You're fucking radiant."

Morgan smiles and looks down. "*You're* radiant. I'm... I just wish..."

"What?" Ari asks.

"I wish I could be more like you."

"Now why would you want to do a silly thing like that?"

Morgan ducks the question and asks one of her own instead. "See you tomorrow in class?"

"Definitely."

Ari brushes a lock of Morgan's hair behind her ear, and when she pulls back her hand she's holding a single peony between her fingers. She hands it to the other woman with a smile and heads back down the hall to the elevator.

"How'd you do that?"

Ari waves without looking back.

She taps her nails along the side of the coffee cup, the trimmed ovals clicking against the thick cardboard impatiently as she waits. She picks up the peony again, running her fingers over the stem, across the leaves, and between each petal as she admires the flower.

"Hey!" Ari calls from the doorway of the coffee shop, crossing through the crowded room. She leans down and kisses her before taking a seat across from Morgan at the small round table.

"Hey! I got this for you," she says, sliding one of the disposable cups across the marbled surface. "It's not the pumpkin one, before you ask."

"Thank fuck," Ari says with a smile, gulping the hot caffeine.

"More for me."

"And I hope you enjoy every sip of it," Ari says, wrinkling her nose as her girlfriend takes a gulp. "You liked the flower I gave you enough to drag it around all day?"

"I'm honestly just trying to figure out how you did it."

"With magic."

"Haha."

Ari tilts her head to one side, raising an eyebrow. "I'm not joking. It's witchcraft. Magic with a capital 'M.' Spellcasting. Whatever you want to call it, that thing you were looking for with the coven last night, that's what I used to make you a flower."

"Come on, stop messing with me."

Ari frowns and pulls the pink peony across the table towards her. She covers the petals with her hands and closes her eyes. After an uncomfortably long moment, she opens them, smiles at Morgan, and lifts her hands to reveal the now black petals. Morgan stares at her, eyebrow raised. Ari covers it once more and closes her eyes. This time, when she reveals the flower, it's a yellow rose. As if to out-do herself, she repeats the process a third and final time, leaving a violet and white lisianthus in her wake.

Morgan stares at the flower for a long time before reaching out to touch it. She moves slowly, like she's worried the plant might bite her, and picks it up delicately. She turns the flower between her fingers before staring at Ari.

"Wow. Just... wow," Morgan breathes, "that's... wow."

"Wow?"

"I mean, what can I even say?"

"Showering me with praise for my awe-inspiring power is always a good place to start," Ari jokes.

"I am in awe of your power," Morgan says quietly.

The other woman frowns and folds her hands in her lap. "Seriously, though, are you okay? Have I freaked you out with this? You seem, I don't know, shellshocked about this. About magic."

"Magic isn't real."

"I thought it's what you were looking for at the coven yesterday?"

"Yeah, I mean, I was," Morgan stammers, "but like? I don't know? I didn't *really* expect to find it. Not really."

"Didn't you, though?" Ari pushes. "Because you seemed pretty let down when you went home."

"I mean, I guess I was a little hopeful."

"So you *were* looking for magic, then."

"Hoping and actively looking are two different things,"

Morgan clarifies.

"Hoping is like the lazy man's version of looking. It's searching for something greater than one's self and assuming you'll come up empty-handed, but that *maybe* you'll find something eventually. And besides, if you're hoping for magic, then it means at least a small part of you believes in the possibility of it."

Morgan drinks from her latte as she digests everything. Eventually, she nods, conceding that there's some truth to Ari's words. She picks the lisianthus up again, looking at it from every side, feeling the petals, and running her hand over the stem.

"Why?" Morgan eventually asks.

"Why what?"

"Why are you showing me this? Why are you showing me magic? Does this make you a witch? Are you going to have to kill me or wipe my memory clean? What does this mean for me?

"Wow, okay, a bit of a floodgate but I'm into it," Ari jokes. She reaches across the table and takes Morgan's hands in her own, holding them gently. "Yes, I'm a witch. And, not to freak you out, but I think you might be one too. I could feel this... energy? Power? *Something* in you when we first met. And it's not the reason I fell in—well—fell for you. I actually thought you knew you had magic, but then you never brought it up, and there was the Wicca date, and I realized pretty quickly you didn't know."

"You think I'm powerful?" Morgan asks earnestly.

"Fuck yes. *And* I think you might have magic, so, bonus," she teases. "So, for your other big questions, I'm showing you magic because if you're a witch then you should learn how to use the gifts you've been given, and know that you don't have to go looking for divinity in other people when you have it inside of you. And if you're not a witch, then I still really like you. Like, a lot. I think I might even," she exhales and gives Morgan a sad smile. "Anyway, I guess I just wanted to share this with you because you're special. And now I kinda hope I haven't freaked you out too much and scared you away forever," Ari says nervously.

"No! Definitely not," Morgan rushes to say, squeezing Ari's hand back. "I mean, yeah, it's a lot to take in, but you haven't scared me with anything. And I like you, too. A lot."

"Really?"

"Yeah, definitely. And, you know, if you're ever comfortable with it, I'd love to see more of what you can do."

"Come on, then," Ari says excitedly, standing up from her chair and pulling Morgan to her feet.

"Where are we going?"

"To make magic."

"You're *so* lame," Morgan chuckles, letting the other woman lead the way back to the apartment complex, the lisianthus left discarded on the table.

The inside of Morgan's apartment is warm and comfortable. A teapot sits on the kitchen counter, Earl Grey steeping inside. On the small living room coffee table, a few candles have been arranged and lit, sage incense burning in a nearby dish. The two women stand with their backs to the mustard sofa, eyes glued to the painting hanging on the wall across from it.

"So, it's going to be hard to access your magic at first," Ari explains, her chin resting on Morgan's shoulder as she stands behind her. "It'll get easier over time and with practice, I promise, but for now it's going to feel like you're trying to reach through a brick wall."

"Sounds fun."

"And yet decidedly not. Lucky for you, I'm going to lend you some of my magic."

"You can do that?" Morgan asks.

"Only to other witches and only if I let you into my heart."

"What do you mean?"

"You'll see," Ari assures her. "For now, just look at the painting on the wall and imagine something *else* was painted on the canvas instead. Think in as much detail as you can. The more specific you can get, the better the results. Once you know what you want, close your eyes and focus your intentions on the canvas."

"Uh, okay," Morgan says hesitantly.

"Don't worry, you're going to suck. Everyone does the first time."

"That's encouraging."

"I'm nothing if not motivational," Ari coos into her ear, "but this is just for practice. I'm more interested in *if* you can cast a spell than if it turns out good."

"Okay."

"You ready?" Ari checks.

"Yeah."

"Okay, I'm letting you in. You should feel it in a second, and once you do focus on the painting."

It doesn't take long for Morgan to feel Ari's energy, and soon her body is flooded with warmth. No, with *emotion*. It's strong and overwhelming, and feels white-hot coursing through her veins and into her heart. It's love and acceptance and *home*. It makes her feel giddy and alive, and she doesn't want the feeling to end. Never again. She can hear Ari whispering in her ear about the painting, and it takes her a moment to focus on what she's supposed to be doing. Eventually, her mind quiets long enough for Morgan to picture a pink galaxy, swirling and effervescent, and she closes her eyes as she pictures every star and beam of light. When she opens her eyes, the colour block painting has been replaced with the rose galaxy that had lived only in her mind a moment ago.

"Wow," Ari breathes behind her, tickling her neck and sending goosebumps running down her spine. "That's… that's fucking incredible." She moves from behind Morgan and crosses the small space between her and the painting. The galaxy is so exact, it could be a photograph. The stars look as though they're expanding into the depths of the ether, the pink gases swirling across the canvas and seemingly off its corners. "I'm serious, Morgan. This is amazing by practiced witch standards, never mind someone's first time. I don't even think *I* could do that."

"Hey, without you it wouldn't have been possible in the first place. It's *because* of you that I was able to realize something this beautiful. Something like you."

Ari smiles at her and closes the distance between them, taking Morgan's face in her hands and drawing her close. As they kiss, Morgan runs her hands through Ari's long hair and to the nape of her neck. She pulls back from the other woman, breathing heavily.

"Did you mean what you said, back at the coffee place?" Morgan asks.

"About?"

"The way you feel about me. Do you really, you know..."

"Love you?"

"Yeah."

"Yeah. I love you," Ari confesses.

Morgan's smile is as radiant as the galaxy on the wall. She kisses Ari deeply and pulls away from her lips before planting another soft peck on her.

"I thought I could feel that from you, but I wanted to be sure. Can I try one more spell?"

"Sure, of course."

Ari puts her hands on Morgan's shoulders and opens her heart back up to the other woman. Morgan's mouth falls open from the high of it as she drinks in the power.

"You need to do something," Ari reminds her, nodding to the photo.

"I already am," Morgan says regretfully.

Ari raises an eyebrow and watches the canvas, waiting for the photo to change. It doesn't. But something inside her does. At first, it feels like a small pressure building within her, but soon she's doubled over clutching at her chest as a searing pain runs through her bones.

"Stop, Morgan, stop! Wh-whatever you're trying to do, stop. I-I don't think it's working."

"It is, don't worry."

"No, please, y-you need to—"

"Calm down, Ari. It's almost over. I'm so sorry, baby."

"What i-is? Wh-y are you sorry?"

"Did you know witches don't have an infinite supply of this shit?" Morgan asks her, trying to lead her first to the couch, and then helping Ari onto the ground as her knees give way. "I didn't. Apparently, it's why witches had covens in the first place, so they could borrow and replenish each other's magic. But for solo practitioners? We just, I don't know, *stop*. The magic goes away, the well runs dry, and we just stop having power."

"Wh-what are you talking a-about?" Ari asks, blinking slowly.

Morgan helps Ari lie down on her side before walking over to the couch, grabbing a pillow, and bringing it back to the woman. She lifts Ari's head and slides the pillow underneath it before brushing hair off the woman's forehead with a delicate hand.

"I'm really sorry you had to fall in love with me to make this work, but you said it yourself, you needed to let me into your heart to use your magic. And an open heart, a *vulnerable* heart, makes tapping into power—draining that power—a lot easier. You *are* an amazing woman though. And you know, in another life, I think we could have worked out."

Ari opens her mouth trying to say something, but another wave of pain rolls through her and she seizes up from the agony of it.

"I hope, in another universe, that we did work out. That we're happy and growing old together," Morgan says.

"Wh-at a-are you t-talking about?" Ari slurs, vision blurring at the edges. There's a pit in her stomach that gets bigger with every passing second, but she's too weak to move. Her breathing is slowing down, her limbs heavy.

"I hope you know how beautiful you really are and how much your strength has inspired me. I hope you know that I wish, *I wish*, this could be any other way," Morgan whispers to her, unaware that all Ari can hear is the blood slowing in her veins. "I'm so sorry, Ari. I hope you know, despite all this, I love you too."

She looks down at Ari's still body with a sad smile, holding her until her body begins to feel cold to the touch. Eventually, Morgan leans over and kisses her on the forehead before closing her eyes and focusing her intentions. When she opens them, Ari's body is gone from the living room floor. Morgan gets up and passes the canvas, chest tight as she looks at the kaleidoscopic galaxy.

Ari stares back, portrait arranged in the painted stars.

.

LOOP

My toes c
around the edge   u
of the wooden beam   r
          l

I s
    w
  a
    y
side
    to
        side
    to
side

The wind p   u   l   l   s at me
tendrils r   e   a   c   h   i   n   g
for me

  s
    w   l
     i   around me
    n   r
  g

But I can't feel ~~anything~~ it

I get ready
It's — almost! — time

The moonlight shines
          through
    m   e

to the water
       f

         a

           r

              below

Any second

             Now

He stands across from me
       on the
B   R   I   D   G   E

He isn't really
                  there
    But I'm not really
here
    But we are.

The fear I'm so used to
OVERWHELMS me

He steps   forward
His heavy footf
    a
    l
     l

s silent

His burning rage
long since
ice cold

He's coming for...
He wants...   me.
He'll hurt...
He can't have...

The man rushes   forward
And I
      jump
         f
         a   f
         l   a   f
         l   l   u
         i   l   r
         n   i   t
         g   n   h   d
              g   e   o
                   r   w
                        n

Until I'm gone
deep below the water
r
o
w
n
i
n
g

The m
    o
    o
      n hangs in the sky

         White light illuminating
         the   bridge that fills the
             g   ap between
then
              and
                         now
here
             and
                      there

I s
   t
   a
   n
   d

waiting

         My toes   c
around the edge   u
of the wooden beam   r
            l

        I s
           w
       a
       y

side
    to
        side
    to
side…

BLOOD AND COFFEE

Laura pulls the sash of the slate grey housecoat tighter before tying it closed. She loves the softness of the fleece against her skin, especially after a hot shower, and she slides her feet into the matching slippers she has waiting for her next to the bathroom door. She runs a hand across the mirror to wipe away some of the steam and checks to make sure her cotton towel is properly secured atop her head. She grabs a tube of chapstick from the ledge of the sink and applies it to her cracked lips before opening the bathroom door. The apartment is cold and even in her thick bathrobe it makes her shiver.

"Good shower?" her boyfriend asks from his seat on the sofa, voice raised.

She smiles. "Yeah, it was really relaxing. It was just what I needed. There's nothing like a warm shower to—"

"Fuck off!" Cody screams into his mic. He kicks the coffee table, frustrated, before disconnecting his headset from his remote. The room, once silent, is now filled with the sound of gunshots and music. The noise is booming, the bass making it feel like the apartment is about to collapse, and she winces in pain from the intensity of the sound. With an exhale that Laura can see but not hear, Cody shuts off his console and powers down the television. "Sorry, what were you saying?"

"Just that the shower was relaxing is all," Laura says. She omits telling him all the unexpected noise has put her back on edge. "I think I'm going to make tea. Want one?"

"No, I'm okay... Actually, could you make me a coffee? Decaf, please."

"Ugh. *Anything* but that," Laura moans, shuffling slowly past the living room and into the kitchen to boil some water. She takes the plastic kettle off its power base, opens the lid, and fills it with tap water before returning it to its spot and clicking the machine on. The inside of the kettle lights up blue and the small kitchen is filled with a low rumbling.

"What's wrong with decaf?" Cody asks, following her into the kitchen and taking a seat at the small table. The old dining set creaks under the weight of him, the hand-me-down furniture hardly able to support its own weight, let alone that of a person.

"Nothing. I'm just tired of making coffee for people. It's all they ask me to do at the office and I'm sick of it. I fucking hate that place."

"Well, I mean, it makes sense that they would ask you."

"What do you mean?"

"Well, like, don't most receptionists take care of that kind of thing?"

Laura stares at him in disbelief, struggling to find the words. "Are you serious right now?"

"What?"

"I'm not a fucking receptionist."

"I thought you answered emails and stuff?"

"*My* emails. *My* stuff. We've been together nearly five years and you're telling me you don't know what I do for a living?"

"Well, it changes all the time!"

"Nope."

"I guess it just feels like you're always getting a new job or a new offer, and it gets hard to keep track of. And like, didn't a company *just* reach out to you a few weeks ago? Like, didn't you *literally* start a new job this week?"

"A headhunter reached out to me, yes, but I didn't start a new job. I've been at this place for like a year now."

"Okay, well then I guess I must have mixed this job up with your last one. Sorry."

"I edited wedding videos at my last job. I'm a content strategist and brand developer at this one. They're kind of hard to mix up."

"Okay, well it's not like you pay attention to what I do for a living, so like—"

"You're a scrum master for a company that specializes in digitizing airplane flight logs."

"Whatever."

Laura crosses her arms in front of her chest and stares at Cody, unamused. He rolls his eyes at her as the kettle screams, the counter rumbling as the water bubbles before there's a loud click as the machine automatically shuts off. She exhales loudly, frustrated like she was before her shower, and focuses on making herself a tea. She drops a small bag of orange pekoe into her plain ochre mug and opens a nearby drawer for a teaspoon. It's empty. She sighs as she turns the tap on, putting a bit of soap on the yellow sponge, and reaches into the sink to fish out a spoon to wash.

"Can you do some dishes while I'm out tomorrow?"

"Sure."

"Promise?"

Laura takes the newly cleaned spoon and scoops some sugar into her mug before pouring the hot water into the glass and giving it a quick stir.

"I said I would."

"Yeah, but you also said you would *today*."

"I know. I know," he says, waving her off with a hand. "You don't have to nag me about it."

She clenches and unclenches her jaw, frustrated, as she takes the milk from the fridge and adds a splash of it to her tea. Cody gets up from his seat at the table and heads back into the living room.

"Oh, don't forget my coffee. Decaf."

Laura rubs her eyelids, the pressure causing stars of white to explode across her vision as she stares at her computer screen. Days with meetings cause her the most anxiety, and given that her boss routinely holds meetings for things that could be said in emails, she's regularly stressed. The clock on her desktop reads *10:27 a.m.* and her stomach drops as she sees it change.

10:28 a.m.

The meeting is now only two minutes away. Her stomach grumbles, her heart beats too fast, and her breathing gets heavier. She feels sweatier, beads of liquid gathering on her forehead and the small of her back.

10:29 a.m.

She closes her eyes as she inhales slowly through her nose and exhales through her mouth.

10:30 a.m.

Her computer dings, the meeting reminder sounding obnoxiously loud in her headphones, and she reluctantly gets up from her desk chair. The plastic wheels roll loudly across the hardwood floors, which creak constantly from age and overuse. She turns off her monitor before grabbing her laptop, a notebook, and a pen—which she tucks behind her ear—before crossing the office to the meeting pod.

Laura hates her office. Everything about it screams "conservative white man trying to make a good impression on naive college graduates desperate for work in content creation and multimedia production." The office is situated in a run-down building that was once low-income housing, before being rebranded as posh apartments that fell victim to time and neglect, which wore them down and made them uninhabitable. The building was then bought for pennies on the dollar by TenByTen Media LLC, the company she works for now, which had invested just enough money to keep the complex standing without ever making it comfortable. Walls that had separated units in the building had been demolished to make way for a "hip" open office floor plan, but remnants of the former apartments still linger. Hardwood floors turn into tile to mark where kitchens had once been, and some of the bathrooms still have showers and tubs installed in them.

Around the office are "pods," as the owner likes to call them. In reality, they're soundproof glass meeting rooms each outfitted with a long table, comfortable leather chairs, a projector with a pull-down screen, and extra bright overhead lights. The boss is always in one of these rooms, although he never does much. He claims that meetings are a great way to get the company's blood pumping and encourage collaboration; in reality, they're a great way for him to snoop on his employees through the glass walls while he sits on display looking busy.

The metal handle is cold against her skin as she opens the door to the meeting pod, the glass walls shaking as it closes loudly behind her. She takes a seat at the long table in the centre of the space, the leather chair creaking as she gets comfortable and waits for the rest of the team to arrive.

"Ever heard of arriving early?" Sean, her boss, says loudly from his seat at the head of the table. He laughs to himself before taking a sip from his black ceramic mug.

"Sorry," Laura mumbles in apology, checking the time at the bottom of the projector.

10:30 a.m.

The room is quiet, the silence punctuated only by Sean's phone vibrating against the desk and his sighs of performative annoyance as he gleefully checks his notifications as they roll in. Laura sits uncomfortably still in her chair, not wanting to look nervous about being in the same room as her boss despite feeling it. Everyone says he's friendly, that he's easy to talk to, but she struggles to find her voice whenever she's around him.

"So, umm, I had an idea for our collaboration with the, umm, the esports people. I was thinking we could—"

"We should wait for everyone to get here before we start."

"Oh, yeah, of course. I just, umm, I thought this meeting was to discuss the branded content we were designing for Tourism Toronto. So I was hoping that before we got started, I could—"

"We'll make time for it at the end of the meeting."

"Yeah. Sure," Laura says, feeling deflated.

She looks at the time on the projector.

10:32 a.m.

10:36 a.m.

10:37 a.m.

The door to the pod opens and a swarm of men enter the space, which suddenly feels much too small. They talk in booming voices and laugh with each other, each taking the time to shake Sean's hand or clap him on the shoulder, before taking a seat at the table.

"Sorry to keep you waiting, Sean!" Antonio, Laura's manager, says with a wide smile and a nasal voice. "I know you're a busy man and I appreciate you making time in your day for this." Everyone nods their head, pretending like they don't remember it was Sean who called the meeting in the first place.

Antonio pulls up a slideshow on his laptop and connects it to the projector before turning off the lights. Images of people smiling in downtown Toronto fill the screen. He opens his mouth, ready to begin, but Sean holds up a hand and leans back in his chair.

"Sorry, just a second," he tells Antonio before looking at Laura. "Could you get us some coffee?"

It's a question, but he's not asking.

Laura stares at him for a moment, choosing her words carefully.

"Umm, perhaps Noel can get it, seeing as I have a few ideas that I'd like to discuss. Besides, what are interns for, right?" She chuckles at her joke, but no one laughs with her.

"They're here to learn, Laura. I think it would be good for Noel to stay and absorb everything from this presentation. Besides, it's a secretary's job to get coffee."

"I'm not a secretary," she says to Sean. *And I think you've mixed them up with waiters*, she keeps to herself.

"Oh. Well," he smiles and raises an eyebrow as if she's in on the joke he's about to tell. "I'm sure you still know your way around a kitchen, right?" The way he casually gives her a once-over before looking at the other men says everything he won't.

The room is quiet, holding its breath.

"Yeah, I'll be right back."

There's a collective exhale as Laura gets up and opens the door to the pod.

"Oh, Laura?"

"Yeah?"

"Can you also run down to the little bakery I like and pick up some pastries?" Sean asks with a wide grin, taking a credit card out from his wallet.

She nods, unable to talk with how tightly her jaw is clenched, and as she leaves the room, Antonio begins the meeting without her.

"They didn't have the ones with the maple and almonds?" Sean asks, making a face and pointing at one of the plain croissants.

"Umm, no. I don't think so."

Sean grumbles to himself and takes a bear claw instead. Antonio, never one for independent thought, takes one too. The rest of the pastries are divided up amongst the meeting-goers as Laura walks around the room pouring hot coffee from the glass carafe into the mugs of her colleagues. By the time she's done, the pot—like her cup—is empty, and the last pastry in the box—the unwanted croissant—is enjoyed by Sean as a second helping.

She brings the empty coffee pot back to the staff lounge and heads back to the meeting. Her feet are sore and blistered, her tan loafers having chafed her pinky toes and the back of her heels raw as she ran to and from the bakery, and she's acutely aware of the sheen of sweat that covers her face. As she approaches the meeting pod, her stomach sinks when she realizes the lights are back on and the projector is off. Noel, Antonio, and Sean are talking amongst themselves, laughing, and she frowns when she begins to see some of her colleagues stand up.

"So," she says awkwardly, pushing a lock of sweat-dampened hair off of her forehead, "what did I miss?"

"Oh, nothing much," Antonio says dismissively before turning his attention back to the other conversation.

"Okay. Well, umm, I had a few ideas for the Toronto Tourism project that I think are worth looking at and—"

"It's okay, we've already figured it out. Noel actually came up with some video ideas we could work into our lineup."

"It's a good thing we sent you out instead of him, eh?" Sean laughs. "We might have missed out on some good ideas otherwise!"

"Yeah. I guess."

Sean leans over and pats Noel's shoulder before pushing himself out of his chair. "Well, good meeting, everyone! Be sure to check your calendar invites for the next one, which I think is—"

"Sorry," Laura interrupts, her heart in her throat, "but you said we could, umm, discuss the content ideas I had for the 4TIS Champion League esports tournament brand collaboration we're doing."

"Oh, that," he waves a hand at her and turns his attention to Antonio, "would you mind going over them with her for me? Unfortunately, I have somewhere important to be."

"No, not at all."

Laura opens her mouth to protest, but the look Sean gives her shuts her up.

"Until next time, everyone!"

Laura is quick to move out of the way, not wanting to block his exit. Antonio smiles at each of the men as they leave the room before turning his attention to her. Although he's still smiling at her, Laura can feel the insincerity of it and knows he'd rather be anywhere in the office than with her.

"So, what did you want to talk to me about?"

She wanted to talk to Sean, but she keeps that to herself. Instead, she takes a seat at the table, opens her laptop, and turns it towards her manager. For a moment, annoyance flickers across his face as he realizes this isn't going to be a quick question, but it's gone in an instant and he takes a seat across from her. She opens a short presentation that she's assembled and runs him through it.

"I was thinking about the 4TIS pitch meeting that we have coming up and how they want to stand out and do something new. So it got me thinking about how we *also* want to do something new. TenByTen has been trying to expand its content offerings since I joined the team and I think this could be the perfect opportunity to fulfill both the client's brief and our portfolio. 4TIS is all about pushing the boundaries of what's expected in the esports industry while trying to make their brand more attractive to the everyday gamer. I know Sean has been talking about entering the reality TV market for a while, but he doesn't really have any premise in mind. You know?"

Antonio nods.

"Yeah, umm, so I thought it could be a cool idea if we held a competition where everyday gamers competed against one another for a spot to participate in the 4TIS Champion League esports tournament. Obviously, there would be a few kinks to work out, but I think it could be an amazing opportunity for—"

"I think it's a cool idea, but it's just never going to work," Antonio says, speaking over her. "It would be costly to produce and—"

"Well, umm, it actually wouldn't be as expensive as you'd think. I looked into the resources we have at our disposal, as well as the assets we can use from 4TIS and—"

"And organizing something this big would be a logistical nightmare—" he says even louder. "It's just not going to work."

"I really think that this is a good idea and I've done a bunch of preliminary work on the concept too, so I was hoping to pitch it at the 4TIS prelim meeting tomorrow and—"

Antonio stands up, all semblance of good humour

gone. "Laura, no," he tells her in the same stern voice you'd use to scold a dog. "This isn't a viable idea and we're done talking about it. Although I'm disappointed that you thought developing this idea was a good use of company time. It makes me question your judgment and just what it is you bring to the team."

He walks around the table and exits the meeting room, the door slamming closed behind him and shaking the fragile walls. Eventually—once Laura is sure she won't cry where people can see her—she gets up from her seat and goes back to work.

Laura stands under the steaming water until she's red like a pomegranate. She closes her eyes and imagines her skin sloughing off and swirling down the drain, taking the events of the day and the shame she feels with it. Once the water begins to run cold, she shuts off the shower, towels dry, and retreats to the warmth of her housecoat. She slides her feet into her slippers by the door, makes sure her hair's secured in its wrap, and opens the bathroom door.

Cody waves at her from his seat, his glass of diet soda balanced precariously on the arm of the couch.

"Good shower?" he asks.

She shrugs. She still wants to curl into a ball, go to sleep, quit her job, and stay in bed forever, but she needs to make dinner and prepare her lunch for tomorrow.

"That's good!" he says.

She looks at him, confused, and realizes he's not paying attention to her. Instead, he's watching a movie on the giant TV across the living room from him. Laura sighs, frustrated, and points to his soft drink.

"You're going to spill that."

"What?" he asks over the noise of the film.

She rolls her eyes and crosses the room, taking the

remote off of the coffee table and hitting the POWER button. The movie flashes to black and the room goes quiet.

"Hey!" he cries.

Laura takes his glass off the armrest and slams it onto a coaster. "*This* doesn't belong on the couch."

"I wasn't going to spill it."

"You said that right before you dropped coffee all over my loveseat. Use the table."

"You don't have to be a bitch about it."

"*What*?"

"You don't have to be so pissy about it," he says. "You seem like you're in a really bad mood tonight."

"Because I *am,* Cody. If you'd bothered to listen to me when I got home you'd already know that."

"I *did* listen. I just thought, I don't know, that you were over it."

"No, I'm not over it. Shockingly, I'm not over being humiliated at work."

"I'm sure it wasn't as bad as you're making it out to be. They asked you to get coffee and some snacks. It's not like they beat you with sticks."

"It's not that they asked me to get coffee. It's that they asked me to get coffee because that's all they think I'm good at. I didn't even get to participate in the project I had ideas for. And the idea I had for tomorrow's pitch meeting is garbage. It's devastating."

"Laura, it's just a job. It's not the end of the world."

"It's not *just* a job. This was supposed to be the start of my career. And instead, it feels like I've wasted my time at a place that only hired me so they could say they had gender diversity in the office. It pisses me off!"

"Okay, well, don't take it out on me!"

"I'm not taking it out on you! I'm annoyed with you for not listening!"

"Well, you're acting all pissy!"

"I'm allowed to be!" Laura shouts at him, exasperated, before heading into the kitchen to get some air.

She breathes in deep through her nose and exhales slowly through her mouth. She rolls her eyes when Cody follows her into the tiny room.

"I just think you're taking this too seriously," he says, leaning against the counter beside her.

Unable to bring herself to respond, she turns on the sink—the dishes still piled high in the basin—and lets the water run from the tap for a few seconds before grabbing the kettle, filling it up, and turning it on. She takes out a teabag and goes to put it in a mug but realizes there are no clean ones left.

"I thought you said you were going to do the dishes."

"I am."

"I thought you said you were going to do the dishes *today*."

"And I *am*."

She rolls her eyes and turns the tap back on, putting some dish soap onto a sponge, before washing a mug.

"Oh my God," he says. "I told you I was going to do them."

"Okay, well I need them done now."

"Just use one of the mugs in the cupboard."

"There aren't any!"

"You don't have to yell at me," he admonishes.

"I'm not yelling!" she says, voice cracking.

She closes her eyes, trying to calm down, and reaches into the sink. She feels her way around the dishes, trying to find a spoon, and she cuts herself on one of the unwashed steak knives propped sharp-side-up against a plate. It slices into her thumb and she shouts in surprise.

"Fuck!" she yells, shaking her hand. The skin is broken and a thin streak of red makes its way down her finger.

"You okay?"

"It fucking hurts!"

"It really doesn't look bad."

"It still hurts!"

"Just be more careful next time."

"Or just wash the fucking dishes so I won't get stabbed when I need something in the sink!"

"You didn't stab yourself. It's a tiny cut. Stop being so dramatic."

Laura's not sure if Cody feels the shift in the air, but she does. Something within her changes, snapping, and before she can take stock of what she's doing she already has the steak knife by the hilt. She turns to Cody and before he can register Laura's intentions, she's plunged the knife into his gut.

She takes it out, the metal utensil squelching, and pushes it back in.

She takes it out.

She pushes it back in.

Over and over and over and over.

Cody falls against the counter and slides against it to the floor. Laura keeps stabbing him until everything is coated in red and Cody is finally still. His chest looks like soggy ground beef and his eyes look up at her wide and accusing. She knows she should care, knows she should be horrified by what she's done, but she doesn't have it in her anymore.

She's exhausted.

She gets up and grabs Cody's arms, dragging him out of the kitchen, through the living room, and into the bathroom. She pushes him into the shallow tub before getting a bunch of towels from the linen closet to soak up the blood in the other room. She's grateful that she lives in a basement apartment and doesn't have to worry about anything soaking through her floor and into the unit below. After she throws the towels into the tub with Cody's body, she takes out her Swiffer WetJet and cleans up what's left of the red. It isn't perfect, but it'll have to do.

She turns the kettle back on, reheating the water that's long gone cold, and turns her attention back to the dishes in the sink.

Sean sits in his usual seat inside, getting up only to shake hands with the executives from 4TIS. Laura watches them through the glass walls from her desk. The pitch meeting is scheduled to begin soon, but Sean has always made a point of fitting in pleasantries before presentations in the hopes that his clients will be more receptive to whatever is being pitched.

Eventually, the clock changes to half-past eleven and Laura gets up from her seat. She takes her notebook and laptop, crosses the open office, and knocks politely on the glass door before opening it.

"Ah, Laura, right on time."

She smiles uncomfortably at him before giving a genuine smile to the two 4TIS executives. She sets her belongings down on the table, but before she can shake their hands, Sean is whipping out the company credit card from his leather wallet.

"What do you guys want?" he asks them.

"I'm fine," the stern-looking one says.

"Coffee, please. Two milk, two sugar," the other tells Laura.

"Perfect. Laura, I want you to put on a fresh pot and bring some mugs for everybody," Sean tells her as the door opens to let more of her colleagues in. "Then I want you to go to that bakery I like and get some pastries. But not the ones you got last time; get the good ones."

It's not a request.

"Oh, umm, I'm actually going to be presenting today so I thought—"

"And be quick about it," he adds dismissively. "Last time you only brought everything when we were leaving. I'd like to be able to enjoy it *during* the meeting this time."

She nods her head and exits the room, blood rushing in her ears.

She balances the box of pastries, cups, and a carafe of coffee on the serving tray she found in the staff lounge and carries everything through the office as fast as she can. Her thumb hurts, the fresh cut throbbing as it rubs against the tray, and the balls of her feet are sore from rushing around in wedges. She's tired and sweaty, and all she wants to do is go home and take a shower but she can't even do that.

Not until Cody has been dismembered and removed from the tub.

She approaches the pod and waits for someone to open the door for her. Although the people inside can see her, no one is quick to help and so she stands outside the door until someone eventually nudges Noel to let her in. He opens it with a smirk.

"Sorry, I didn't see you there," he lies.

She wants to spit in his face but swallows her frustration instead.

"That took you long enough!" Sean barks as she sets the tray down beside him. He goes to take a pastry before thinking twice and offering them to the 4TIS executives first. Laura pours a cup of coffee into one of the mugs and passes it to the friendlier of the two men. As she does, she catches a glimpse of the presentation on the projector.

"*DO YOU HAVE WHAT IT TAKES TO BE THE NEXT 4TIS CHAMPION LEAGUE WINNER?*" the projector reads.

"What is this?" Laura asks.

"The project Antonio will be spearheading with 4TIS. It's a reality show to find the next esports champion."

White spots appear at the edge of her vision and her skin feels too hot.

"That's my idea. You took my idea," she tells her manager, who has the decency to at least look uncomfortable. "You took my idea after *you* said it was shit."

"Calm down, Laura. He made sure to mention that you helped him come up with it."

"I didn't *help* him come up with the idea. *I* came up

with it on my fucking own."

"We can talk about this later," Sean tells her, waving a hand to both silence her and encourage Antonio to keep going.

"Why is he leading it?"

"Laura—"

"Why is he leading my fucking project, Sean?" she says, breathing heavily.

"We can discuss this after the presentation. I'm so sorry about this," he tells the executives. "She's not normally so—"

"Why is he leading my fucking project?" she screams.

The room is still as Sean and Laura stare each other down. Eventually, he breaks the uneasy silence. "Because I thought he could handle it. I don't know that you can. And given your behaviour today, it wasn't the wrong call."

"*My* behaviour? You treat me like a waitress and let this asshole steal my idea and you're complaining about *me*?"

"Stop being so dramatic."

She feels it again, the smallest spark coming to life, igniting her rage. The carafe of boiling coffee comes down onto Sean's head before she has time to think about what she's doing. He screams as the glass breaks against him, shards from the pot tearing into his skin while the hot liquid burns and blisters his skin. He panics and flails in pain, trying to get up from his chair and away from Laura, but she's thrown herself on top of him before he gets the chance. The two of them— chair and all—crash onto the hardwood floor.

The room is in chaos. Everyone is screaming and fleeing for the exit while Sean wails from the ground. Laura brings the broken carafe down onto his face, hard, his nose crunching as Laura breaks it and his skin tearing from the jagged glass. She lifts it again and brings it back down. This time, the force is enough to lodge a piece of glass in his cheek and crack the plastic rim that keeps the handle on the pot. Sean struggles back, hitting Laura in the process, but this only enrages her more.

She lets go of the broken carafe and gets up, grabbing her laptop from the table. She can hear the muffled cries of people watching her through the soundproof glass, but she doesn't care. She turns back to Sean—now crawling blindly across the floor—and brings the metal laptop down over his head. There's a loud crack from his skull and he falls flat on his face, blood spattering the walls and Laura. He rolls himself onto his back as she lifts the laptop back over her head and he holds up his arms to defend himself from the oncoming blow, but it's no use. She swings the computer and he screams as the device awkwardly strikes his wrist, breaking it at an angle. She straddles him and beats him with the machine again and again and again.

Laura hears the door open behind her and an authoritative voice yells at her to drop the "weapon" and lift her hands above her head.

She doesn't.

Instead, she brings the laptop down on what used to be Sean's face one last time before she's tackled to the ground by an officer.

As she's handcuffed, she watches happily as Sean gurgles and coughs, choking on blood and coffee from the hole in his face that used to be a mouth. His teeth are chipped and missing and his jaw has been so badly caved in that it looks like his tongue hangs limply from an angry gash. His nose is gone, obliterated, as are his cheekbones. His eyes are swollen shut and whatever skin isn't covered in blood is burnt.

Laura smiles, that sense of calm settling in like it did last night, and she lets the officers lead her through the office while paramedics rush in to fight a losing battle. She locks eyes with a few familiar faces as she moves through her former workspace and catches a few snippets of conversation before the front door closes behind her.

"I can't believe it. How could she—"

"—too emotional—"

"—always so quiet—"

"And you're saying it was the receptionist who attacked him?"

THE AMPHITRITE

She looks at her watch—*5:22 p.m.*—and sighs. Six o'clock feels so far away, even though it's right around the corner. She can hardly hide her frustration at having to wait, and she quivers in anticipation as she looks out of the giant observation windows, trying to spot approaching lights in the dark water. Soon, a fresh crew will be here to relieve her of her duties aboard the Amphitrite. Soon, she'll be allowed to go home.

It's only been a few weeks that she's been aboard the observation base, but for her, it feels like months. She'd jumped at the chance to join the crew when the university had approached her with the opportunity. Her mother had always joked that marine biologists seldom became famous and so Emilia had hoped this journey would prove her wrong. The enclosure had been built as part of an international initiative to observe, document, and record the impact that global warming was having on ocean life. The Amphitrite had been a technical feat like no other and was designed to accommodate crews of up to fifteen people for weeks at a time. The station was fixed to the ocean floor, was able to synthesize its own oxygen, and even had a docking bay so submarines could bring supplies and researchers as needed. It was everything Emilia had ever dreamed of as a child.

At least until she boarded it.

She shivers and tries to rub some warmth into her arms, hoping to shield herself from the omnipresent chill. It's one of the things she hates most about the station, along with the dampness that gets into every corner. It doesn't matter where she is in the vessel, be it her room or the observatory, the cold follows her around.

She looks into the sea and frowns at the darkness of the water. This far below the waves, she seldom sees the sun. At first, she didn't mind, the excitement at being part of the crew was enough to sustain her, but now she misses the warmth overhead and the baby blue of a cloudless sky. She resists the urge to roll up the sleeve of her black turtleneck and check her watch again, and instead looks into the water and twirls her long black braid between her fingers.

The room is massive and made entirely of glass. It used to be her favourite place in the station when she first arrived, but now the view of the endless black makes her feel hopeless. Alone. She misses the laughter of her crewmates and conversations with them in the cafeteria. It's been so quiet since... she's not entirely sure. There were eleven other people on the research team with her, but she struggles to remember where they've gone.

Something moves behind her, its reflection warped and blurry in the glass. She closes her eyes and tries to take a calming breath, but instead, she feels like she's drowning. She grabs at her throat and struggles to breathe, the sensation of water cold on her tongue. She opens her eyes and looks down at the crystal clear floor, tucking her shaky hands into the pockets of her jeans as she steadies herself. It isn't the first time she's imagined this *thing* in the darkness with her, but somehow it feels more real each time she sees it.

Emilia watches a crab scuttle through the nearby rocks before it stops suddenly, waiting as a school of fish rushes by before continuing its journey. She watches the crab move, fascinated with its fat body, as her breathing returns to normal.

She looks at her watch—it's only *5:22 p.m.*—and tries not to groan with frustration. If only it was six o'clock, she'd be on her way home. She misses the smell of fresh air and watching green plants sway in a summer's breeze. Nothing grows down here in the ocean's twilight zone, not with so much of the sun filtered out during the day and nothing but emptiness at night. She looks out the window and tries to remember what it feels like to have grass under her bare feet and the scent of blooming lilacs on a summer's breeze. It's hard for Emilia to recall anything but the wet and the cold of the Amphitrite. It never used to be so noticeable, but ever since the rest of the crew... *left?*

The word doesn't feel right.

They were supposed to be going home today, too. They'd been speaking about it only a few days ago and all of them had been so excited for today's departure at six. She doesn't understand where they could have gone.

Something moves behind her again, its reflection distorted in the glass. It's pale and hovers at the opening of the room, tendrils of black hair swirling around its face. Although Emilia can't make out many details from her spot by the glass, she can see its dark bulbous eyes watching her from the back of the room. It stares back at her for what feels like an eternity before turning away and hovering out of the room and down the hall.

She stays motionless for a long time, holding her breath until her throat feels impossibly tight and her lungs hurt. She keeps her eyes glued on the spot in the darkness behind her, waiting for the thing to make its way back, but it never comes. She opens her mouth to ask the crew if they saw the creature too, but closes it once she remembers that she's alone.

But she shouldn't be alone. She looks at her watch— *5:22 p.m.*—and tries to remember if the crew said anything about heading ashore before her six o'clock departure, but nothing comes to mind. She looks out into the depths of the ocean, half expecting to see the empty eyes of the thing staring back at her, and tries to recall the first time she saw the ghostly being aboard the station. When her mind draws a blank she closes her eyes, ignoring the sensation of icy water in her throat and pressure in her chest, and concentrates. Emilia remembers them being excited to leave, she remembers them gathered near the docking bay waiting for... she's not sure. She remembers them panicking, worried, something over the intercom about a hatch, and then nothing. The memory fades to black and all that's left is the wet and oppressive cold of the

Amphitrite.

The thing is back.

It stands in the doorway of the room, its back towards her, and waits. Emilia watches its reflection in the glass, breath catching in her throat, before turning to look at it. It hovers between the ceiling and floor, not touching either, and its arms rest at its side. Its plain jeans and black turtleneck look discoloured and frayed at the edges, its feet bare and blue. It moves slowly back into the hall, dark hair floating like a blackened halo around its head, and moves out of view.

This time, Emilia follows it.

She feels heavy and her movement is laboured and slow, as if the air around her has turned thick and solid. Outside the glass, fish swim by and shadows move through the dark waters. Emilia follows them with her eyes as she crosses the massive space, finding it hard not to get caught up in the mystery of the ocean just outside the walls. It's why she's always wanted to study marine life.

Most people thought that the next true adventure for mankind was deep in the galaxy, but she knew the real adventure was deep in the sea. Her parents had been so proud of her when she'd announced that she would be one of the first researchers to board the Amphitrite, and had even called her the next Sylvia Earle. They had bought her a beautiful new watch to mark the occasion, with a silver face and leather wristband. Her father had joked that while it was meant to celebrate her deep-sea accomplishments, she couldn't get it wet. *To our dearest Emilia*, the engraving on the back read, *may this help you keep track of the hours until we see you again. We love you so much. XOXO. Mom and Dad.*

She can't wait to get back to them. Soon, she'll be on the transport that will take her up to the surface. She looks at her watch—*5:22 p.m.*—and smiles at the thought of the sun on her face and her parents' arms wrapped tightly around her. If only six o'clock would get here sooner.

She stands in the centre of the room and tries to remember what she was doing, but her brain feels foggy and the specifics evade her. She looks around the empty space, the silence unsettling. *The crew should still be here... why aren't they?* Suddenly it clicks and she remembers what she was going to do: find where the rest of her team went.

She moves to the doorway and stops in her tracks as tendrils of black peek out from around a corner down the hall before disappearing out of view.

The thing is back.

She desperately wants to run away, but something inside her forces Emilia onwards. She moves slowly towards where she last saw the spectre, her feet noiseless on the metal flooring of the hall. She holds her breath, shaking from the fear and from the cold of the Amphitrite. Her skin is wet and uncomfortable, and she's not sure if it's from sweat or water. She turns another corner, the hall opening up to reveal one of the many work labs aboard the station.

The thing stands motionless ahead of her, back facing Emilia. It looks wrong and the familiarity of it makes her shiver. The thing hovers with its arms and legs limp and splayed out. Up close, its bare hands and feet look more black and purple than blue, with patches of white peeking through the discolouration. The clothing it wears looks uncomfortably tight and restrictive, as if the material has shrunk or the thing has grown. Its black hair floats lifelessly, part of it still done up in a long braid. On its wrist is a watch with a silver face and a leather strap. It's a watch that Emilia recognizes.

"Who are you?" she asks.

When the thing doesn't answer, she reaches out and gives it a push. It turns slowly, bobbing awkwardly in the flooded room, and Emilia's too scared to scream when she sees her own face looking back at her. Its eyes—*her* eyes—are open, colourless, and bulge from their sockets. Her face is bloated and frozen in a silent cry, her lips swollen and her tongue lolling between them. Her skin is marked by decomposition, with some patches red and sloughing off, others black and marbled with blue veins.

She backs away from her waterlogged body, grabbing

at her throat as her mind remembers the icy cold that forced its way into her lungs when the hatch of the docking bay broke. She had been in the observation room, taking in one final look at the sea, when the water had flooded the vessel. She remembers the pressure inside her body, the burning deep in her chest, and the scared faces of her crewmates through the glass as their bodies were swept from the Amphitrite and into the black of the ocean.

She turns on her heel and runs, putting as much distance as she can between herself and the body. She can feel her empty eyes watching her as she flees, and feels them on her long after she's run from the hallway towards the safety of the glass room. She sinks to her knees, sobbing, and presses her forehead against the cold glass. She watches the shadows beneath the floor of the observatory, losing herself in their rhythmic movement and the flashes of colour slowly becoming visible as daylight begins to make its way through the deep waters.

She runs a hand over her face and is annoyed to find her cheeks wet. She hates how cold and damp everything is aboard the Amphitrite. She looks at her watch—*5:22 p.m.*—and smiles. It's almost six o'clock. Soon, she tells herself, she'll go home.

23 MCCORMICK ROAD

ONE

Everly stares out the window of the Toyota, the houses and trees all blurring together in the dim glow of the yellow streetlights. She knows she should be excited, but after a long day of driving, she's mostly just tired.

"We're almost there!" Brooklynn says excitedly as she turns down a street that looks just like the last street.

"You said that when we pulled off of the highway ten minutes ago, Brooke."

"Yeah, but now we're *really* almost there. Look, we're just passing the depanneur you thought was cute."

Everly leans closer to the glass, squinting as she looks out into the dark. As promised, the small mom-and-pop corner store stands before her, with its white brick walls and a boxy yellow aluminum awning that hasn't been changed since the fifties, even if it has been painted several times since. Its glass windows are cluttered with signs promising everything from fresh milk delivered daily to the best soft-serve ice cream in town (which the realtor admitted is only available in the summer but is, in fact, some of the best ice cream around). Although the proximity of the corner store certainly hadn't been the main selling point for them, Everly had spent a strange amount of time fantasizing about going for walks as a family to get treats on a hot summer night.

"We're only a few streets away."

"Yeah," Brooke confirms.

Everly sits up straighter in her seat and feels a little more awake. Although she's dead tired, she finds her second wind as the SUV cuts a path to their new home. They turn a corner and this time she recognizes the street, the giant mustard yellow house on the corner an unmistakable landmark indicating that they're close. Brooke takes a right at the end of the road, making sure to take the turn wide enough to accommodate any parked cars and the U-Haul trailer hitched to the back of the RAV4, and slowly drives up McCormick Road. Everly holds her breath in anticipation as Brooke whispers the addresses under her breath.

"Seventeen… nineteen…"

Everly reaches out a hand and puts it on her wife's thigh. With a smile, Brooke takes one hand off of the steering wheel and puts it on top of Everly's, lacing their fingers together.

"Twenty-one…"

She eases onto the brake, stopping in front of 23 McCormick Road. Everly smiles; the house is just as beautiful under the night sky as it was in the daytime sun.

"Son of a bitch," Brooke hisses.

"What? What's wrong?"

She motions to the elm in the front yard, frowning. Beneath the massive tree is a pile of rusted metal: the bones of an old car long abandoned.

"They said they were going to clear it off of the property before we moved in."

"Maybe they forgot."

"They shouldn't have; it was in the purchase agreement."

"We can call Michael tomorrow and get it figured out. Let's just get in, I'm exhausted."

Brooke nods and takes the SUV out of park before

backing it, and the trailer, into the driveway. Once the engine is turned off, Everly is quick to unbuckle her seatbelt and open the door, enjoying the cool night air on her skin. She slowly gets out of the car, holding her stomach as a familiar pain shoots through her lower abdomen. She exhales slowly through her mouth, holding onto the door frame for support as she breathes through the discomfort, before stretching her arms over her head to work out the kinks in her back. Her tailbone and lower back hurt from sitting all day, a fact Brooke is acutely aware of as she stands behind Everly, rubbing small circles on her back with the palm of her hand.

"You doing okay?" she asks, already knowing the answer.

"I'll be fine once I get a nap in."

"You don't need a nap, you need a full night's sleep," Brooke tells Everly, kissing the back of her shoulder. "Are you sure you don't want me to book a hotel for the night?"

"I'm sure."

"I just don't feel like you're going to get much rest on an air mattress."

"It'll be fine."

"And, like, how are you even going to get onto the floor in the first place, let alone sleep comfortably? I'd really feel better if you let me—"

"How am I going to get on the floor?" Everly says, laughing. "How big do you think I've gotten?"

"We both know that's a trap."

"I'm only fourteen weeks along, not thirty," she reminds the other woman, running a hand over her stomach. "It'll be fine. Plus, I want to be here when the movers arrive tomorrow morning, not stuck across town eating scrambled eggs from a box at a lukewarm buffet."

"That sounds delightful."

"Not when you have morning sickness."

Brooke makes a face at the thought before nodding in agreement with her wife. Once Everly is ready to move, Brooke closes the car door and helps lead the other woman across the luscious front lawn, up the steps of the porch, and to the front door of their new home.

"Ready?" she asks, taking out the set of keys from the front pocket of her jeans.

Everly nods, holding Brooke's hand tight with her own as she first unlocks the deadbolt and then the front door, before pushing it open to reveal the inside of their home. They stare at it for a while before Brooke finally speaks.

"That was a bit anticlimactic, wasn't it?"

Everly starts laughing.

"I don't know what we were expecting. It's an empty house in the middle of the night that we've already seen."

The two of them chuckle to themselves as they step over the threshold, not bothering to turn on any of the lights. There are no curtains on the big bay windows and the soft glow of starlight, the moon, and the dull lamps from the road streams into the space.

"I'm an airhead tonight," Brooke says, slapping her forehead with the fleshy part of her palm. "I forgot the mattress and sleeping bags in the car. I'll be right back."

"Want some help?"

"No, no. I'll meet you upstairs."

She heads back to the truck as Everly climbs the staircase next to the foyer. She runs her hand up the smooth bannister, enjoying the way the polished wood feels under her skin as she climbs to the second storey. She opens the door to the small bedroom on her right and sets her purse on the ground by the window. The room is eventually going to be the nursery, but tonight it'll be their makeshift bedroom as they wait for the movers to arrive with the rest of their things tomorrow.

Downstairs, the front door closes softly and the locks click into place as Brooke returns with their things. She huffs and puffs up the stairs, stopping in front of the open door with an armful of their belongings. Their overnight bag is slung across her shoulder and two sleeping bags, a box holding an air mattress, and a compact air pump balance dangerously high in her arms.

"You didn't want to sleep in the master bedroom tonight?"

"Well, I figured since we're going to be sleeping in that room for the next twenty years—"

"Our mortgage is for thirty," Brooke mumbles.

"—then we should enjoy this one for at least tonight," Everly says happily, crossing the room to help unburden her wife.

Together, they blow up the air mattress, unzip the two sleeping bags into two massive blankets, and change into their pyjamas before crawling into bed together. Everly lies on her side and smiles as Brooke wraps an arm around her, pressing the warmth of her body against her back as she rests her hand gently on her stomach.

"Goodnight, babe. Love you," Brooke mutters.

Everly isn't sure if she even answers as she slowly drifts to sleep.

The last thing she remembers seeing is the face of a small boy watching her from the hallway.

TWO

"No, Michael, you said it would be gone by the time we arrived and it's still here," Brooke complains into her cell, pausing to listen to the realtor on the other end. She balances the iPhone between her ear and shoulder as she picks up one of the boxes from the trunk of the U-Haul and carries it across the lawn. "Okay, but that's *really* not my problem!"

She glances at Everly before rolling her eyes dramatically, her classic "can you believe this guy?" look, before heading into the house with the box of cleaning supplies, her voice fading from earshot.

Everly smiles to herself, feeling sorry for whoever's going to catch Brooke's ire, as her eyes rove over the shell of what used to be someone's car entangled in the elm tree. The frame is rusted; what she imagines used to be smooth silver metal is now rough copper, with holes on the old frame and gaps from where the rust has curled up or flaked off. Despite the obvious dents and bends in the metal indicating that the car had once been in a serious accident decades earlier, Everly can still make out the telltale signs of a Volkswagen Beetle. The gulf blue flecks of paint that have managed to cling to the rust bucket are bleached from the sun, and although she's no expert in vintage cars it looks like something straight out of the sixties.

Despite how much of an eyesore the front of the car is, the back half is less visually upsetting to Everly on account of the fact that it's hidden by the massive elm tree that's grown around the vehicle. Thick roots have pulled the back tires into the ground, the bricks the tires were once resting on have fallen to the side, and sturdy branches grow through the back windows and out through the front ones. The metal of the trunk and part of the cab look like they've been swallowed by the trunks of the elm that wrap over and around the vehicle.

It's an eyesore, which is why photos of the elm and its accompanying Beetle had been left out of the online listing. The sight had been a surprise to Everly and Brooke when they'd made the drive out to visit the property in person all those months ago.

"Then I really hope you have his number!" Brooke shouts into her phone, ears red with frustration. "Fine, bye," she says, failing to sound polite before closing the lock screen and stuffing the phone into her back pocket.

"And?"

"And I'm going to wring Michael's fucking neck," she spits.

"So I guess he's *not* getting a crew to haul the car away then, right?" Everly asks with a sardonic smile.

"WELL," Brooke starts, voice raised, "apparently they can't remove the car without cutting down the tree."

"Oh, but I *love* this tree."

"Well then I guess you're gonna be jazzed when I tell you that it's protected by the city and that we're stuck with the metal heap because of it."

"Why?"

"Apparently, it's a heritage tree."

"A what?" Everly stares at her wife blankly.

"Apparently the tree was planted in, like, the sixties or something in memory of a boy who went missing. So if we want to cut the tree down, we need to get a bunch of signatures supporting our request—preferably including the Mayor's—and then we need to petition the city council to hear our case and *then*, if they like us enough, they might agree to have the fucking thing cut down."

"Well, that's bullshit. You said it was in the agreement we signed when we brought the property, so don't they have to honour that?"

"Apparently it's a promise the guy couldn't make, so no."

"Well… we can't just cut through the metal to free the car?" Everly asks, as she reaches up to twist her hair into a messy bun. The morning is warm with the promise of an early summer, and between the sun overhead and the extra heat from her pregnancy, she's starting to feel like she's melting.

Brooke shakes her head. "Michael said the guys who came to haul the car a while back said it was so badly tangled with the tree that there's no way of getting it out without damaging the elm."

"And if we just say 'fuck it' and cut the tree down ourselves?"

"Then we're going to get a massive fine and up to a year of jail time."

"Oof… good thing the baby only needs one mom, I guess," Everly says.

"True… I'll make sure to tell them about you every single day," Brooke laughs. "Honestly, though, if I'd known we'd be saddled with this pile of rust when we bought the house…"

"You'd, what? Not have bought it?" Everly asks.

"I'd have made a lower offer."

As the two of them laugh in the driveway, a massive white truck pulls to the side of the road, blinkers on, before the engine shuts off and two men get out of the cab and round the back of the vehicle.

"I guess that's my cue to get cleaning."

"You really don't have to," Brooke insists. "I mean, what was the point in hiring professional cleaners if you're just going to do the work a second time?"

"I'm not doing heavy labour, babe. I'm just going to be sweeping up any rogue dust, wiping down a couple of counters. It's fine."

"You should be taking it easy. I'll go clean, you can order the movers around."

"I thought you wanted me to take it easy?" Everly laughs. "You know watching people move things stresses me out."

"Okay, so then kick your feet up and enjoy the morning and I'll delegate and clean," Brooke says, leaning in to give her wife a kiss.

Everly wraps her arms around Brooke's waist, pulling her close. She's hot enough that she can feel her hair sticking to the sweat on the back of her neck, but she still enjoys the warmth of the other woman against her.

"How about I clean for a bit—"

Brooke rolls her eyes, dissatisfied with Everly's insistence on working. "You really don't—"

"—and then, when you're done bossing the movers around, you come boss me around too?"

Brooke breaks into a small grin, eyebrow raised. "*Fine*, but promise not to push yourself, yeah?"

"Promise," Everly says, holding up a hand and crossing her fingers.

Brooke sighs and kisses Everly first on the lips and then on the forehead before stepping out of the other woman's hold. She crosses the lawn and approaches the workers as Everly watches her, pointing at things in the back of the truck and motioning to a stack of paper in the driver's hand. A bead of sweat rolls down the side of Everly's face and she wipes it away with the back of her hand, the sun suddenly feeling hotter than it did a few minutes ago.

Everly retreats into the house, kicking her running shoes off by the door before crossing the hardwood birch flooring to the kitchen. She turns on the sink, letting the water run cold, before she gathers some up with her hands and drinks deeply. She repeats the process twice more, then cups her hands under the water and splashes her face and presses her cold wet hands against the back of her neck. She leans over, letting the excess water drip off into the metal farmhouse sink, suddenly remembering that she hasn't unpacked any towels.

She watches the water drip slowly onto the metal, each droplet exploding into a bunch of smaller ones as they make contact with the hard surface. As she stares, Everly becomes acutely aware of the feeling that someone is watching her from the entranceway of the kitchen. She straightens back up and turns around, the last few droplets running down her skin and under the neckline of her lilac t-shirt. She searches the doorway, but it's empty. She runs her hands over her jeans to dry them as she searches for whoever must have just been at the door.

"Hello?"

She moves out of the room and into the dining area, then through the hallway to the living room, but the house appears to be empty. When she spots Brooke and the movers through the window, still negotiating the contents of the truck, she tries to shrug the feeling off and heads back to the kitchen.

The kitchen is big and airy, like the one in the house her grandparents used to own when they were still alive, and she smiles to herself as she imagines her child growing up in a house so much like the one she'd spent her summers in long ago. Her parents, both in big law, had always worked long and tedious hours. Although they'd scheduled their vacation during her summer break, they'd still worked more than they were ever at home. Thankfully, her grandparents had both taken an early retirement, and so her summers were spent with them in their suburban house while her parents had remained in the city.

Everly opens one of the cardboard boxes that Brooke has stacked on the counter and frowns. She was gung-ho to clean only a few minutes ago, but in the short time she's been indoors she seems to have lost her enthusiasm. She searches the empty kitchen, eyes finding the broom and dustpan leaning against the door to the backyard. She quickly sweeps up the living room and dining area, making sure to corral the dust out of the way of the movers as they tread through with the sofa. They place it on the floor and head back out the front door, their shoes laying fresh dirt back onto the clean floor.

Everly sighs to herself and returns the broom to the kitchen, deciding to sweep once everything's been unloaded from the truck and the U-Haul trailer has been unpacked. She takes a roll of paper towels out of the cardboard box on the counter and tucks a bottle of Windex under her arm before heading upstairs. Although she's given up on sweeping the house until the movers leave, it doesn't mean she can't clean the medicine cabinet mirror or the windows.

She starts with the room furthest from the stairs on the second storey: the master bedroom. She sprays the windows with the blue liquid and wipes them with the paper towel, removing flecks of dust from the nearly spotless glass. This room is massive, big enough to fit both the office and bedroom from her last apartment, and she's excited to see what the space will look like once she and Brooke have finally finished settling in.

In the bathroom, Everly wipes down the mirror on the front of the medicine cabinet that's built into the bathroom wall. Although the house has undergone a fair number of renovations and updates since its construction, there are still a few parts that show the building's age. The rusted car on the lawn is one of them, and this medicine cabinet—with its built-in slit for at-home razor blade disposal—is another. Once she's satisfied with her work, she wipes down the windows in the room that will be her new office, and then enters the last of the upstairs rooms: the soon-to-be nursery.

That's when she feels it again.

The familiar prick of eyes on the back of her neck, her hair standing at attention as goosebumps form across her skin and down her arms.

She turns around, expecting to see Brooke or one of the movers watching her, but she's alone on the second storey balcony. She looks over the railing, wondering if maybe they're staring up at her or trying to get her attention from the base of the staircase, but the men are lifting the bottom half of a plastic-wrapped china cabinet as Brooke leads them through the hallway to the dining room.

Everly tries not to linger on the feeling as she returns to the nursery. She crosses the space to the windows, spraying Windex on the glass. As she runs the paper towel over the window, she realizes there are fingerprints on the glass.

They're small and dark, like someone was playing in dirt before opening the window for some fresh air, and they reach only as high as the bottom of the glass panel.

When she's done cleaning the first window, she moves onto the second one and frowns at the tiny finger prints that cover the bottom of the sill and the glass. She traces her finger through one of the prints, smudging the dirt on the window, and shakes her head. She's not sure what she was expecting, and she rolls her eyes at herself as she squirts more of the blue cleanser onto the window. She is just tearing off another sheet of the paper towel when she hears the sound of glass cracking.

She looks up fast and is surprised to find that the bottom of the window is cracked. Deep lines are etched into the glass, spiralling and radiating outwards. She traces one of the lines with her finger, accidentally cutting the tip of it on the sharp edge of the pane. She hisses and drops the paper towel roll onto the floor.

She puts the tip of her finger in her mouth and tastes copper as she watches the paper towels unravel as they roll across the hardwood before suddenly stopping, like the roll's bounced into something.

She stares at the empty spot on the floor, breath trapped in her chest. She slowly pans upward and sees them looking back at her.

A set of brown eyes.

Everly recoils in surprise, backing up against the window and dropping the spray bottle of cleanser. It hits the ground hard, dragging her gaze down for a split second before she quickly looks up again, frantically searching for the staring eyes that are already gone. The paper towels continue to unroll across the floor and she leans against the glass to catch her breath, the back of her shirt damp from the cleanser that's still on the window.

Once she's finally calmer, she rolls the paper towels back around the cardboard tube, picks up the Windex, and finishes wiping down the window. It's only as she rubs the last of the cleanser off the glass, her index finger throbbing, that she realizes the cracks in the glass are gone. She stares at her finger, wondering if she'd imagined the whole thing, but the paper-cut-thin tear in her flesh is clear as day.

She stares out into the front yard, trying to collect her thoughts as she watches the two movers enjoy a smoke against the side of the truck.

"How's it going up here?"

Everly jumps, clutching a hand to her chest as she spins around to face Brooke in the door.

"You okay?" Brooke asks, crossing the room to her partner.

"Yeah, I just—"

Saw a ghost?

Saw eyes?

Lost my mind?

"...You surprised me, is all," Everly eventually says. "Sorry. I bumped into Windex."

She puts the cleaning supplies down on the floor and peels off her t-shirt, tossing it onto the ground. She pulls out another shirt from the overnight bag and pulls it on.

"Are you sure you're okay?" Brooke asks again.

"Yeah, I'm fine."

"Alright, well, do you have a second?"

"Sure, what do you need?"

Brooke begins to lead Everly out of the room and back down the stairs, and the other woman lets her, eager to be out of the nursery. As her wife talks to her about the placement of kitchen hutches, Everly does her best to push the nursery encounter from her mind. She fights the urge to look back as she feels eyes on the back of her neck, watching her descend the stairs.

THREE

Everly leans against the railing of the balcony, letting the wind whip her hair around her face as she looks over the edge of the porch and down into the grass below. The movers have been gone for the last few hours, having unloaded both the truck and the U-Haul Everly and Brooke had towed with them (for a bit of extra cash, of course). Although their previous apartment had been small, they'd packed it full of all the things they'd need for their new home. Before deciding to buy a house, the two had invested in all new appliances and an updated bedroom set. After they'd signed the contract, they added a new sofa, big TV, and a dining set to their growing list of big purchases. Once all this furniture had found its rightful place, all that had been left was to sweep out the dirt that had been tracked into their house and to unpack the seemingly unending stacks of boxes that had been piled in the rooms of their new home.

Although she didn't do any lifting, the day's move was exhausting for her. Wherever she'd gone, she could feel eyes on the back of her neck, watching her as she worked. She'd found herself spending most of the day looking over her shoulder as she unpacked their belongings and tried to figure out where things should go, while being distracted by someone who wasn't really there. More than once she'd jumped out of her skin thinking the pair of floating eyes were back, only for them to suddenly be gone when she'd tried to get a good look at them.

As the day had worn on, it had only gotten hotter. Even with the windows open and the breeze helping to air out the big house, Everly had found the heat suffocating. Now, she stands on the porch with her eyes closed, trying to calm her nerves and ignore the sensation of sweat running down her back and wetting her face as she breathes deeply.

"It's never fun, is it?"

Everly opens her eyes, surprised to find an older woman only a few feet away, smiling at her from her front yard.

"What?"

"Moving. It's never fun, is it?" the woman repeats with a smile. "But damn does it feel good once you're finally settled."

"I'll let you know if we ever get to that point."

The wrinkles around the woman's eyes and mouth from years of good humour and kind smiles grow more pronounced as she chuckles. She wears a pair of linen pants dyed tan, a sage long-sleeve shirt, and a pair of brown Birkenstock clogs. Her curly grey hair hangs to her chin and is pushed off her face so that Everly can see the tortoise-shell pattern on her glasses.

"I'm Patty. I live next door," she says, nodding to the house on the left of theirs.

"Everly," she says, coming down off the porch and extending her hand to the older woman. "My wife's named Brooke."

"Yes, I had the pleasure of meeting her earlier this morning!"

"Oh, I'm so sorry," Everly jokes.

"I'm not!" Patty laughs. "It was refreshing to hear someone use such, uh, *colourful* language to describe a car."

Everly laughs as she stares at the Beetle across the lawn.

"Yeah, I can imagine. She's not thrilled we're stuck with it."

"You can blame Dillon's father for that one."

"Dillon?"

"Sorry, Dillon Matthers. He was the previous owner of this place."

"Ahh, right. Sorry. Baby brain," Everly jokes. "So

you're saying his dad is the one Brooke should be mad at?"

"Yes," Patty chuckles. "From what I remember Dillon saying, his father got into a hit-and-run but didn't have insurance. So he kept the car, insisting he'd get around to fixing it, but he never did and then, well..."

"And then the elm grew," Everly finishes for her.

"Exactly. Dillon would go on about how funny it was when his dad complained about all the shit that he'd been hauling in his trunk that he'd never be able to get out since the damned thing had gotten jammed in the crash."

"Oh, that sucks."

"A real bitch, ain't it?"

Patty smiles and Everly is surprised by how genuine it is. It's not the uncomfortable grin of a polite neighbour trying to make friends, but one that shines with sincerity.

"I know you only just got here, but how are you finding the place so far?"

Everly knows it's not meant that way, but it feels like a trick question given the day she's had. She thinks about the eyes in the nursery, the feeling of someone observing her all day, and she shifts her weight uncomfortably from foot to foot. She chooses her words carefully before answering.

"It's been an adjustment. I'm not used to the place yet, but I'm sure it'll feel like home soon."

The older woman nods.

"I'm sure it will. I mean, Dillon spent his entire life there."

"It's too bad we never got to meet him. We dealt directly with the realtor representing his kids, I think."

"I'm betting they represented his extended family. Dillon didn't have any kids when he passed away. He didn't even have a wife."

"Really?" Everly asks, crossing her arms over her chest. "It seems like a big house to want to live all alone in."

"Well, truth be told, I don't think Dillon ever felt alone in the place. It was his family's home and I don't think he felt like he could ever really leave," Patty admits.

"Oh?"

"That house has a gravity to it." Patty smiles, but this time it doesn't quite reach her eyes. "But what old house doesn't?" she asks, attempting to lighten the mood.

"Yeah. I guess."

There's a weight to the air between them now, and Everly picks a stray piece of lint from her jeans. Behind her, the front door opens and Brooke steps out onto the porch.

"Hey! Patty, right?"

"Yes! Hello again!" the old woman says, tone happy once more. "I was just passing by to invite you both to dinner at my place, once you're all settled in. Instead, I talked your wife's ear off."

"That's so sweet of you! I can't wait to take you up on that!"

"Great! Give me a shout and we can pick a date that works for you."

"Sounds good!"

"It was nice seeing you again. And it was nice meeting you, Everly."

"You too," Brooke answers for the both of them.

With a wave, Patty crosses the lawn back to her place. She gives a final smile and head nod once she gets to her front door, before heading inside.

"I'm going to return the U-Haul to the depot. I'll be back soon."

Everly looks up at the empty house, the hair on the back of her neck standing to attention.

That house has a gravity to it.

"Can I come with you?" Everly asks. "It'll give me an excuse to see more of the neighbourhood."

"Sure! Need anything from inside before I lock up?"

Everly shakes her head, not wanting to go back into the building just yet. With a smile, Brooke locks the front door before taking Everly's hand in her own and leading her to the car.

FOUR

Everly sits on the edge of the bathtub, the translucent curtains pushed open as she leans over and fiddles with the temperature, turning the plain silver knobs mounted on the white tiled wall this way and that as she tries to get it just right. The water tumbles out of the faucet, cold droplets splattering against the side of the porcelain-enameled basin as the too-cold water quickly becomes too hot. She turns the knob a bit to the left, keeping the tips of her fingers in the water as she finally gets the temperature just right. She grabs the rubber stopper and blocks the drain with it, letting the tub fill up while she lights some candles on the counter next to her glass of non-alcoholic rosé.

Despite all the progress she and Brooke have made in unpacking boxes and rearranging their belongings, the house at 23 McCormick Road has yet to feel like home to her. Although her wife has been adjusting well to the move, there is something about the house that still doesn't sit right with her, herself. Although she has yet to see the floating brown eyes again, she still feels like she's under constant surveillance. No matter which room she's in or who she's with, she feels like she's always on display and always being followed in the old house.

"Maybe you're just homesick?" Brooke had offered when Everly first admitted how she's been feeling in their new house.

"Homesick? For our old tiny two-bedroom apartment that cost an arm and a leg and always had something wrong with it?"

"Yeah."

"Why would I be homesick for a place I was excited to

move out of?"

Her wife had merely shrugged.

Unsurprisingly, that was also the last time she'd brought up her anxieties about their house with her partner. Brooke has always been a skeptic, never someone to put stock in anything she can't see or rationally explain. Everly has always thought it's a cute trait, laughing whenever Brooke dismisses well-meaning people who guess her astrological sign or tell her they've seen a ghost. But now that Everly is on the other end of it, she doesn't find it funny at all. She finds it frustrating.

She pulls the elastic out of her hair, shaking the tight braid loose with her fingers, before she steps out of her clothes. She throws the t-shirt in the bathroom hamper along with her underwear and jeans, but hangs her bra on the back of the door to wear again tomorrow. It's her favourite one because it doesn't cut into her shoulders or irritate the skin of her constantly changing body.

She looks at her body in the reflection of the mirror, the amber glow of the candles making her eyes look hooded and her skin look pale. She runs a hand along the red scars that have started to weave their way up her belly and over her sides, stretch marks beginning to take root in her body even this early into the pregnancy. She's excited to be a mother, but she can't help but wonder if her dreams of a quiet suburban life have tied her to a house she no longer wants.

She grabs an extra towel out of the linen closet, hanging it up on the nearby towel bar, before turning her attention back to the bath, frowning when she sees the water.

In the candlelight, it looks like blood.

She flicks the switch on the wall, squinting as her eyes adjust to the sudden bright light. The water is murky, brown, and smells like pennies. Her heart beats fast as she attempts to reason with herself: it's not blood that fills the basin, but water from rusty pipes in need of cleaning. She turns the tap, the water getting hotter and spewing out more rust, before the tawny liquid eventually runs clear once more.

Everly breathes slowly through pursed lips, feeling her quick pulse slow to normal. She opens the cabinet under the sink, pulls on a pair of bright yellow gloves, and grabs a bottle of bathroom cleanser and a rag. She turns off the tap and she reaches into the water to unstop the tub. She sits on the rim of cold porcelain, watching as the brown liquid slowly swirls down the drain, before bending down to clean the tub. She knows that Brooke would protest if she were home—*You shouldn't be cleaning! And you* definitely *shouldn't be touching any chemicals, Eve!*—but she desperately wants to relax in a bubble bath and doesn't want to wait for her wife to get home to wipe away the leftover rust from the tub.

Once she's sure the porcelain is clean, she runs the water once again and pours in some bubbles, watching to make sure that the water doesn't turn orange, before putting the stopper back in the drain. She strips the rubber gloves off, dropping them into the empty washing machine to take care of later, before turning the lights off once more and letting the glow of the candles softly fill the space. She puts her glass on the floor beside the bathtub and climbs into the warm water, letting it crest over her body as she relaxes into the bubbles, the tip of her stomach just starting to poke out.

She imagines what she'll look like at five months, at seven, at nine, and smiles to herself at the thought of her swollen body. She lets the steam from the hot water fill the bathroom, the eucalyptus scent of the soy candle washing over her as she gives herself permission to relax and let go. For the first time in days she feels completely alone, and she basks in the privacy that she didn't realize she was craving.

She sits in the water for a long time, her skin wrinkling and the tips of her fingers puckering from the moisture. She doesn't realize she's closed her eyes until she eventually bats them open, the light of the candles and their reflection in the mirror brighter than she remembers. The bath water is cold and her back is stiff from the hard porcelain, and it takes Everly longer than she wants to admit to sit up in the tub. The ends of her hair are wet and stick to her chest and the back of her neck.

She grabs the ledge of the tub, ready to pull herself out, when she sees them.

Footprints on the tiled floor.

Footprints that stop right next to the tub.

Footprints that are too small to be her own.

Everly's breath catches in her chest as she tries not to panic. She tries to remember if she or Brooke have mopped the bathroom since the move. If they haven't, then the same person who'd left the markings on the window could easily have left these footprints behind too. But if they have…

A shiver passes down her spine and she tries to blame it on the rapidly cooling water.

"Is someone here?" she finally manages, hoping that no one answers her back in the darkness.

The room stays silent.

"Hello?"

She's not sure why she asks, why she keeps prodding, but she holds her breath as she waits for someone to say anything.

Nobody does.

She lets out a sigh of relief and finally stands up, the water sloshing around the basin as she moves. Her body hurts, a familiar pain running up her spine and down into her hip as she gets to her feet, and she grimaces as she puts a hand on her lower back for support. As much as she enjoys being pregnant and knows she'll mourn the feeling when it's gone, she won't miss the body aches and pains.

She steps out of the tub and onto the cold floor, droplets of water rolling off of her body and onto the tiles below. She moves carefully on the slick ceramic, making a mental note to buy a bath mat the next time she's at the store, before reaching for her towel. She dries her body with the soft cotton, before flipping her hair over and wringing it out with the towel. Water rains onto the floor around her as she dries her hair, and her heart sinks when she notices that the only dry spot on the ground is where the footprints are.

She breathes slowly through her mouth, praying it's

just a bad coincidence as she dips her fingers in a nearby puddle on the floor. With her heart hammering in her ears, she flicks the water at the footprints, trying to prove to herself that it's nothing.

The water doesn't hit the ground.

Instead, it lands on something her eyes can't see before rolling slowly downward and beading onto the floor.

Everly puts a hand over her mouth to keep from screaming as she watches the footprints turn towards the door, trailing water across the tile in the shape of little feet. As she stares at the ground, her eyes welling up, she hears the bathroom door open and the sound of the feet padding away.

Everly stays bent over for a long time before she eventually sinks onto the cold wet floor of the bathroom and sobs into the towel.

FIVE

Brooke crosses her arms over her chest as she looks at the pile of rust, her frown deepening with each idea that Everly rejects.

"Maybe if we dump enough chemicals on it, the thing will just fucking die on its own."

"Probably, but so would the grass and anything around the tree. And if there's rain, something might run off into the neighbour's yard and kill their plants. Not to mention we have no idea what will happen to the soil itself," Everly says bluntly. "Plus, when our kid is finally born, we don't want them accidentally playing in anything we might have contaminated or—"

"I get it! I get it!" Brooke huffs. She takes her baseball cap off and slaps it against her leg.

While the hunk of rusted Beetle has been bothering Brooke since they moved into the house, the situation came to a head the other day when the wind had blown her favourite pride flag off its pole, across the yard, and into the pile of rusted metal. Despite her attempt to dislodge it from the wreck carefully, the flag—which had gotten snagged on the edge of the passenger door—had ripped beyond repair.

Everly, on the other hand, has been too preoccupied with the incident in the bathroom to care about the car in the front yard.

"What if the tree 'accidentally' caught fire?" Brooke offers.

"And what if the 'accidentally on fire' tree decides to take the entire neighbourhood down with it?" Everly counters.

"Then let's hope the city has a shit fire chief and that everyone else has great insurance."

Everly laughs and puts a hand on her wife's shoulder,

in part to comfort her and in part because she's tired of standing in the warmth. Despite it still being spring, the area has been suffering from a heatwave like none other and she's missing the cooling comfort of the house's central air. Outside, the air is thick with humidity and hot enough that her skin feels sticky and slick with sweat. It makes her miserable and short tempered, but for Brooke's sake, she's been trying her best to stay in high spirits.

"What if we just… left it?" Everly finally says.

"You don't want the kid to play in a pile of chemical waste but a pile of rusted metal that junks up the yard is fair game?"

"Technically, it's not a heap of rusted metal, it's a rusted *car*. And, no, I'm definitely not advocating that we let them play in it. But what if we just worked around it?"

"What do you mean?"

"Well, like, people do cool things with old cars all the time, right?"

"I guess."

"They find ways of reusing them or turning them into something new. And since we already have a tree growing through the middle of the car, it might be cool if we just turned the whole thing into this weird, artsy, wildflower garden."

"You want to make the rust heap a garden?"

Everly tilts her head to the left and squints at the blue Beetle, ignoring the rust and the patches of dirt around the tires where the grass won't grow as she pictures it all bursting with flowers and life. She imagines the hood open and the space that's currently occupied by an engine instead filled with dirt and flowers that spill over the edges, attracting honey bees. She imagines a bird feeder hanging from a branch of the elm, robins and blue jays trying to collect food before the squirrels get to it first, small hummingbirds fluttering between the flowers for nectar and drops of dew. She smiles to herself as she imagines their child running over green grass and ant hills, chasing a butterfly around the old Beetle, a small white fence around the base of the car keeping any danger at bay while they play.

She nods to Brooke. "Yup. I want to make the rust heap a garden."

"Do you think anything's going to be able to grow with all of that rust?"

"Well, I mean, the tree did just fine."

"Yeah, but that's a tree."

"True. But maybe if we fill the car with enough dirt and put some kind of a liner to keep the tree roots from interfering with the roots of the plants it'll be fine?"

"And if it's not?"

Everly runs a hand through her hair and clicks her tongue against the back of her teeth. "Then we'll have spent a lot of money to turn the rust heap into a dirt pile, which I think would still be an improvement."

Brooke frowns at the Beetle.

"I mean, if that's what you want to do, we can give it a try. I just wouldn't get your hopes up that it's going to work out like you want."

"It's worth a try. Especially since the alternative is leaving it here for—"

There's a knock from inside the car that stops Everly mid-sentence. She holds her breath, waiting to hear it again, until Brooke finally speaks.

"You okay?"

"What the fuck was that?"

"What was what?"

"That knocking sound."

"*What* knocking sound?"

"You didn't hear it?"

"No, I have no idea what you're talking ab—"

Everly holds up a hand, silencing Brooke as the knocking starts again. It's low and muffled, but clear enough that she knows it's coming from the car. Someone is rapping their knuckles forcefully against the old metal. It happens a few more times before stopping again.

"That! That's the noise I was talking about!"

"I didn't hear anything, Eve," the other woman says with a frown. "Are you feeling okay?"

"Am *I* feeling okay?" Everly asks, dismayed. "How did you not hear that?"

Brooke shrugs, confused. "I don't know, I just didn't hear anything."

The knocking starts again and Everly gestures to the car for Brooke to listen. The other woman does, her eyebrows scrunching together in concentration.

"Do you hear it now?"

"No, nothing," Brooke says. She looks her wife over, brow still furrowed with worry. "Are you sure you're okay?"

Everly rolls her eyes and approaches the Beetle, gently placing her hands on the hood of the car as the dull banging noise continues. Although she can still hear the incessant knocking, she doesn't feel any vibrations. She runs her fingertips along the frame of the car, making sure not to press too hard over jagged edges or flakes of lifted rust. She doesn't want to give herself a splinter or accidentally cut her hand open, but she's desperate to find where the sound is coming from. As she approaches the middle of the car, stepping over roots and dodging branches, the knocking gets louder and she swears she can feel something pulsating under her hand.

"I think it's coming from the back seat... no, wait," Everly says, sliding her hand further back. "It might actually be from the trunk. I think."

Brooke approaches the Beetle from the opposite side, coming to face her wife. "I don't hear anything, Eve."

"Put your hands on the car, you'll feel it."

Brooke rests her palms flat on the side of the trunk. It's hard for either woman to get a good grip on the vehicle thanks to the sizable elm swallowing it up, but they persist nevertheless.

"I don't feel anything except the looming threat of hepatitis, Eve."

Everly shakes her head, annoyed, her hands pressed against her side of the trunk.

"It's coming from here. The knocking. I can feel something slapping the metal from back here."

"I really don't feel it."

"So then it's probably in this corner."

Brooke rounds the tree and puts her hands next to Everly's.

"I feel like I'm going nuts. I don't feel anything, *at all.*"

"I don't know what to tell you. It's plain as day to me."

Everly grabs the handle of the back door and pulls, trying and failing to open it. She grabs the handle again and pulls, leaning back on her heels as she tries to rip the door free. Instead, the rusted handle breaks apart in her fingers and she goes flying backwards. Thankfully, Brooke is there to catch her before she can crash into the hard ground.

The knocking stops again.

"Careful!" Brooke shouts, steadying Everly on her feet.

"Thanks."

"What were you thinking?"

"I was just trying to open the door and then it got stuck," she says, dropping the rusted handle onto the grass next to the Beetle. "I think an animal might be stuck in the trunk or something. It would explain the knocking, you know?"

"The knocking only you can hear."

"Yes, the knocking only I can hear," Everly sighs. "We need to get the trunk open to at least check."

"I don't think that's going to be possible, Eve," Brooke says, pointing to the back half of the car.

The elm, like most old trees, has grown massive in the years that it's been left to its own devices. The branches are wide and thick, with some of the lower ones growing through the back window of the car where there was once sturdy glass. The branches reach through the cab, filling the inside of the car with green, and out through where the windshield should have been. The two small windows in the back seat of the car have long been shattered, and the one next to the passenger's seat is cracked, but the driver's seat window is miraculously intact. The trunk of the elm has wrapped around the trunk of the car, swallowing the back end of the formerly gulf blue Beetle.

"Well, maybe if we get the back doors open it'll be enough to scare out whatever animal is hiding in the trunk. And if not, we can always try cutting a hole through the back seat or something."

"Or something," Brooke mutters.

"We can't just leave it there."

"Sweetie, I'm sure if an animal did get in, it'll be able to get out, too. We're probably just scaring it."

"You can help me get it out, or you can keep out of my way as I try," Everly says, bracing one hand on her hip and using the other one to caress her stomach. It's not subtle, and Brooke is smart enough to know that it's a feeble attempt by her wife to make her feel guilty, but that knowledge doesn't protect her from the gesture's desired effect.

"Oh my God, fine, *fine*. I'll get my tools," Brooke huffs, heading back across the emerald lawn to the house. "Don't try anything while I'm gone! With your luck, you'll accidentally impale yourself on rust or break your leg on a root."

Brooke continues to mumble to herself as she walks out of earshot and Everly rolls her eyes, watching her other half disappear into the open garage.

The knocking from inside the trunk starts again, and she can't help but be drawn to the car, resting her hands on the body of the old vehicle. She wants to reassure whatever animal is trapped inside that everything is going to be okay and that it'll be out soon, but she knows there's no way of communicating this information in a way it'll understand. So, instead, she admires the old car as she waits in silence for Brooke to return.

She soon finds herself staring at the cracked passenger's side window, her eyes tracing the spider web pattern in the glass, losing herself in the lines. The feeling that she's stuck in a spider's trap creeps into the back of her mind.

She shakes her head, chuckling at her over active imagination, and that's when she finally sees them.

The eyes reflected in the window.

She leans against the car for stability as she stares back at the eyes, her legs feeling weak and her mind racing. The eyes watch her unblinkingly in the glass and she struggles to think, to breathe, to stay standing. The banging from inside the car gets faster, harder, like the animal knows Everly's not alone with it.

She watches as the eyes in the window get bigger.

Not bigger, she realizes. *Closer.*

Long black lashes and dark brown brows come into focus, a face materializing before her very eyes. A small nose, full lips, and those too-big eyes sit in a small heart-shaped face framed by unruly brown hair and a soft chin that just reaches the bottom of the car's window frame. It takes her a minute before she realizes that she's not looking at the face of a grown man, but of a little boy.

"Oh," she whispers, involuntary.

The boy's eyes widen in surprise before his face disappears in a blink, his eyes the last things to vanish from the reflection.

The banging from the trunk stops, only this time there's a weight to it. A finality.

"No, don't go!" Everly shouts, taking her hands off of the car and whirling around to try to find the boy, but it's no use. There's no one left in the yard except for her.

"Don't go?" Brooke calls from the garage door, toolbox in hand as she crosses the driveway, headed back for the yard. "I've been gone for like fifteen minutes already."

"I'm not talking to you." Everly walks around the car, careful not to trip on any roots as she circles the vehicle, desperately looking for anywhere the child could have run off to.

"Well then who *are* you talking to?"

"The boy."

"What boy?"

"I don't know! I saw him in the window. He was the same one from the bathroom and the nursery and he was out here looking at me from the car and now he's gone!" She drops to her hands and knees to look under the car, her heart racing. It's pointless, especially since the back wheels have sunk deep enough into the earth that there are only a few inches between the rusted frame of the Beetle and the hard ground. But still, she checks under the rusty car before Brooke's sturdy hands help her up.

"There was a kid in the bathroom?"

"No, well, maybe. I mean, he was invisible but he was there."

Brooke stares at her with concern plain on her face, keeping a hand on her wife's back as she gently leads her away from the car.

"What are you doing?" Everly asks, looking back at the Beetle and its quiet trunk.

"Getting you inside."

"But we need to go and check for the—"

"Later. We need to get you out of the heat."

Everly knows what her partner is saying, even if she's not speaking the words out loud.

The sun is getting to you.

You're imagining things.

I'm worried about you.

I think you're going crazy.

"Yeah, okay," Everly finally says. She walks slowly across the lawn, letting Brooke lead her into the cool house.

As the door closes behind her, she swears she can feel the boy watching her from the car once more.

SIX

"You know, the point of me inviting you over for supper once you were settled from the stress of moving was to save you the stress of having to feed people," Patty jokes as she takes a seat at the dining room table.

"True, but having you come over forced us to *finally* unpack our dishes," Everly admits, waddling out of the kitchen with three empty wine glasses. Patty moves to rise to help her, but the pregnant woman shakes her head and waves her off with her free hand as she places the stemware at each seat. "We desperately needed someone to light a fire under our asses."

"Well, I'm happy I could help, but next time it's on me," Patty says with a wide smile.

Brooke follows Everly into the dining room carrying two bottles. She fills her and Patty's glasses with red wine before filling Everly's glass with sparkling pear juice.

"Thanks, sweetie."

Brooke smiles and gives her a quick peck on the lips before carrying the bottles back into the kitchen.

"So, how have you been liking the house?"

It's not meant to be a loaded question.

"It's been... fine, I guess?" Everly says, trying to sound nonchalant.

"You know, people normally sound excited when they talk about what it's like to own their first home," Patty says, taking a sip of her wine. "So I'm guessing 'fine' is code for 'not great.' What's got you down? More repairs than anticipated?"

"No, the house has been shockingly well cared for, actually. Like, we're under budget for pretty much everything so far," Everly admits. "I'm really surprised."

"If you'd known Dillon, you wouldn't be. That man

loved this house more than anyone's ever loved a home."

"Oh," Everly says, wetting her dry mouth with a sip of her sparkling juice. "I think you mentioned that this house was in his family, right?"

"It was, yeah. Dillon once told me that this entire neighbourhood used to be farmland and that his parents bought the house before it was built, back when developers started converting this area into the cozy suburban hamlet that it is now."

"So you weren't kidding about it being his family's house."

"I wasn't," Patty says with a crooked smile. "But you still haven't answered the question: what's wrong with the place?"

"Well, nothing's wrong with it," Everly says, squirming uncomfortably in her seat.

"Then what is it?"

"Everly keeps seeing things," Brooke says candidly as she comes back into the dining room. She balances the three dishes carefully on one arm, an old habit from her time in the hospitality industry, and sets them down as she rounds the table to take a seat next to her wife.

"What kinds of things?"

"It's nothing, really," Everly says, trying to shut the conversation down.

"A kid, I think. And eyeballs? But those belonged to the kid, right?" Brooke asks her partner.

Everly sighs, embarrassed by the turn the conversation has taken, and nods.

"Really?" Patty asks earnestly.

"Yeah. I, uh, I felt something upstairs and then saw these eyes staring at me when we first moved in. And then it happened again when I was taking a bath."

"Most recently, she saw a kid outside by the car on the lawn," Brooke chimes in.

"It was probably just the heat, or the stress of moving, or the pregnancy or something," Everly says quickly, wishing the three of them were talking about anything else.

"Or," Patty starts, running a hand through her hair and avoiding Everly's eyes, "it's Dillon's brother."

"What?" Brooke and Everly ask in unison.

"Dillon's younger brother, Zachary, went missing when they were kids," Patty explains, sipping her wine. "When Dillon was still around, he was convinced he could see his brother in the house."

"Really?" Everly asks, surprised.

"Yeah. I mean, I chalked it up to his mind going early, but he was seriously convinced that Zach was still around. Maybe he still is," she says with a shrug.

"What happened to him? To Zach," Brooke asks. "Did they ever find out?"

Patty shakes her head sadly.

"No one knows. He and Dillon were playing hide-and-seek and he just never came home. Some people thought he ran away, some thought he was kidnapped... there was a search party and everything, but they never found him."

"That's *horrible*," Everly says, placing a hand on her stomach protectively.

"Yeah."

"Did Dillon have any ideas as to what happened, or..."

"Not really. I mean, when he told me about it, he was really insistent that Zach hadn't run away. Apparently, they were a really close and happy family, so it never made sense to him that people thought his brother had just run off. But other than that, he never really went into much detail about it. But, you know, Dillon thought his baby brother was haunting their family home. So I can't imagine he thought Zach was still alive."

"Guess not," Brooke says somberly.

Everly looks down at her plate, her eyes tracing the rose and vine pattern that runs along the edge of the china. She prods her food with her fork, rolling a carrot lazily past the chicken breast and into a small pile of mashed potatoes.

"Did Dillon ever say what Zachary wanted, you know,

after he passed? And did he say if his, uh, ghost," she cringes at the word, feeling a bit ridiculous talking about spirits and hauntings with a woman she barely knows, "was friendly?"

Patty scrunches her face in thought, taking another hearty sip of her drink.

"When I moved in next door with my now ex-husband almost twenty years ago, Dillon was already pretty old, so I didn't take much of what he said about Zach seriously," she confesses. "I remember him saying that Zach was lonely, and stuck, and just wanted to play. But that's pretty much everything I remember about him. Everything else was in one ear and out the other."

Everly nods and looks down, scooping some potatoes onto her fork and shoveling them into her mouth. She wishes Dillon were still around so that she could ask him more about his brother and what happened the day he went missing. She wishes she could ask him what kept Zach from scaring him so badly, and if the boy's presence ever went away for more than days at a time. She hates feeling like she's never alone in her house, like she's being followed all the time, like she's being watched when she's by herself.

"More wine?" Brooke asks Patty, changing the topic.

"Yes, please!"

Brooke goes to get up from her seat at the table, but Everly holds up a hand, stopping her.

"I'll get it."

"Oh, sweetie, I don't mind—"

"I want to. I think a little walking around is what my body needs right now," she insists, supporting herself with one hand on the table as she gets to her feet. In truth, she needs a minute to be alone, she wants to clear her head, and she's suddenly so hot she needs to shove her face in the freezer. She gives her wife a small smile and exits the dining room as Brooke and Patty continue to eat in comfortable silence. She's happy to see her partner getting along so well with their neighbour—although it shouldn't be much of a surprise since Patty reminds her so much of Brooke—but she can't help but focus on the news of Dillon's missing brother and the possible ghost loose in her house.

Everly opens the fridge and leans in, closing her eyes as the cool air chills her face. She never used to be so warm, but the pregnancy has her running hotter than the sun. She tries not to think about how stuffy her body is going to feel in the mid-summer heat as she takes out the sparkling juice. She grabs the bottle of red off the kitchen counter and waddles back to the dining room, circling the table to refill everyone's drinks. She glances back at the kitchen, debating if it's worth it to bring the near-empty bottles back, before Patty interrupts her internal struggle.

"At the rate your wife and I are drinking, you should probably just leave the bottle," she laughs.

Relieved to not have to walk back, Everly sets the bottles down on the table and takes a seat. She watches happily as Brooke and Patty continue to chat about everything and nothing while they enjoy their meal. She picks up her drink, savouring the way the cold glass cools her hand, and takes a sip.

The second the liquid hits her tongue, she realizes something is off. She spits the liquid back into the glass, mouth puckering and face twisting from the taste.

"What the fuck?" she cries, grabbing her cloth napkin and wiping her mouth, the liquid dripping down her chin and onto the front of her dress.

"Babe, what's wrong?"

Everly gestures to the glass, horrified.

"What?" Brooke asks again, confused.

"I just got a mouthful of-of-" she stops, struggling to find the right words before it hits her. "-rust. I got a mouthful of rust."

"A mouthful of rust?" Patty repeats.

"Yes! Smell it!" she holds up the wine glass, passing it over to Brooke who stares at her with concern.

She brings the mouth of the glass to her nose and smells it, shaking her head. "I don't smell anything but pears."

"Taste it, then!"

Brooke lifts the rim to her lips, taking a small sip.

"Eve, it's just juice," she says slowly.

Everly stares at her in disbelief before turning to look at Patty, who frowns uncomfortably.

"You don't smell it?"

"The rust?" Patty asks.

"Yeah."

"No."

Everly runs a hand through her hair, pushing it off of her forehead as she closes her eyes. She's warm again, too warm, and she breathes slowly in an attempt to cool off. When she opens her eyes, her heart threatens to jump out of her chest.

The boy is back.

She sees him in the reflection of her glass. He watches her, unblinking, as she stares at his face in the liquid. She wants to turn around, to see him face-to-face, but she's afraid that if she moves he'll disappear again.

"Eve, are you okay?" Brooke asks.

Everly doesn't want to answer, worried she'll scare the boy away. She keeps her eyes locked on him in the glass as she whispers to Brooke.

"He's here."

She holds her breath, expecting the apparition to disappear, but he continues to watch her in the glass.

"Who?"

"Don't you see him? He's right behind me."

Brooke looks behind her wife and then back at Everly.

"Sweetie, there's no one there."

Deciding it's worth the risk, Everly slowly turns to face the boy, deafened by the sound of her blood pumping through her veins. She blinks, trying to figure out why she can see the hallway behind him when it hits her: she's looking right through him.

He's smaller than she was expecting, with thin arms, gangly legs, and a body that hasn't caught up with his stretched out limbs. He wears a pair of dirty white Chuck Taylors and a white t-shirt tucked into a pair of Levi's with dirt on both knees. His curly brown hair is unruly and sticks up at odd angles, and a smudge of grime dirties the tip of his small nose. He watches her with his large doe-like brown eyes and she smiles at him, trying to be brave.

"And who are you?"

His bottom lip quivers and he takes a step away from her, his figure starting to fade.

"Are you Zachary?" she asks.

He slowly comes back into focus, looking clearer but none more solid as he nods his head.

"Hi Zachary, I'm Everly. It's nice to finally meet you. But I've seen you before, haven't I?"

He nods again.

"Who the hell are you talking to?" Brooke asks loudly. She starts to rise from the table, but the other woman puts her hand up quickly, trying to reassure the small boy with a smile.

"Don't, Brooke. Nobody move. *Please*, nobody move."

Zachary watches the three women with apprehension, open and closing his hands anxiously.

"Where's Dillon?" he finally asks.

Everly frowns, not sure how to answer the question. She settles on a gentle version of the truth.

"He's not here anymore."

"Where is he?" the boy asks again, shifting his weight from foot to foot. His eyes begin to well up.

Everly wishes she had something comforting to tell him or that she knew how to answer him better.

"I don't know."

"He was supposed to find me, but he didn't."

"I'm sorry to hear that."

"And now I can't go find him until someone finds me."

"That sounds really tough."

"I wanna find Dillon," the boy says, starting to cry in frustration.

"I know you do, sweetie. But—"

"I wanna find Dillon! I wanna find DILLON! I WANNA FIND DILLON!" he screams over and over, getting louder each time.

His voice is booming, louder than any noise she's ever heard, and she puts her hands to her ears as he screams. She opens her mouth to say something, but she knows it'll only get lost in the noise and so she closes her eyes and begins to fold in on herself, dropping to her knees, her head pulsating like it's going to explode. Something shatters at the table and Everly screams from the pressure between her eyes.

A hand grabs her shoulder and the noise stops.

"Everly?"

She breathes fast and hard, trying to clear her mind as Brooke and Patty help her to her feet. She feels exhausted and her head hurts, a migraine having taken root at the back of her skull.

"Everly?" Brooke asks again, her grip on her wife's arm getting tighter.

"I'm fine. I'm fine. Sorry."

"What the fuck happened?" Brooke asks.

"He was here. The boy, Zach, he was here. He was looking for Dillon."

The two women stare at Everly, worry lining their faces.

"Sweetie, I think we should get you to the doctor," Brooke says, gently cupping her face. "You've been seeing things and hearing things, and now this..."

"I'm not going crazy."

"I'm not saying you are! But this stress can't be good for the baby, and who knows if maybe these, uh, hallucinations are a sign of something else."

The dinner table catches the corner of Everly's eye, and she turns around to observe the damage, leaving Patty and Brooke standing awkwardly behind her.

"I just think—" her partner continues, but Everly points to the place settings, cutting her off.

"How do you explain that?"

The other women approach the table, the silence thick between them as they try to rationalize what they see.

Everly's wine glass is broken, thin lines spiralling and swirling to form a spider web across the surface of the thin bowl, and rust-coloured liquid leaks out of the cracks and spills onto the table.

SEVEN

Everly tries to move, but she can't. Her arms are bound at her sides, her legs free to kick but unable to do anything useful, and she can feel it getting harder and harder to breathe each time she tries to pull oxygen into her lungs. Sweat drips off her forehead, the salt stinging her eyes, and her skin feels like it's bubbling in that familiar summer heat. The room around her is black, and she desperately tries to remember how she got there, but it's impossible.

That's how she realizes it's just a dream.

She sighs in relief, body relaxing even though her chest stays tight and sore.

She looks around the space, shapes beginning to come into focus, but she struggles to make sense of them. She watches as branches slither across the ground towards her, getting thicker as they get close, splitting at the ends over and over and over, replicating themselves until it feels like they're going to swallow her up.

There's a flash as bright light cuts through the green, the warm glow of sunlight just out of her reach. She knows it's too far for her to touch, but she's compelled to try as she reaches an arm out and grabs at it, trying to collect handfuls of sunshine.

The room fades to black again and when the light comes back, it's softer and brings with it the gentle glow of stars. She tries to count them, but they blur and bleed together and she watches them slowly fade from view as she's submerged in blackness once more.

Water starts to drip down her neck. It's uncomfortably cold and smells like pennies. Soon, it's raining on her in the black and she wants nothing more than to find cover, but she can't move. Her arms are bound once more and her legs are ineffective and she tries screaming with lungs that are on fire as water slowly fills the space around her.

And, just as quickly as the rain came, it's gone.

"He was supposed to find me, but he didn't," she says into the void. "Why hasn't he found me?"

She kicks her feet and struggles against whatever it is that binds her, panic beginning to well up inside her once more as she struggles to breathe.

"Let me out!" she screams.

Only, she doesn't scream. She can't. She doesn't have the air.

She kicks her feet wildly, beating them against the ground as she writhes and sobs and suffocates. She can feel the pressure around her waist tightening and constricting. It feels like it's going to cut her in half, and she wishes it would just stop because it's too much. It's all too much. It was supposed to be a game, a stupid game, and now she's *stuck*.

She opens her mouth to scream again but tastes only rust and dirt and oil. Something moves in the darkness with her, scuttling over her body and onto the ground somewhere below. Another insect moves in the darkness, laying eggs and eating filth as she screams into the void that's become her tomb.

She kicks her legs, lungs like fire as they stop taking in air.

The water is back and she hears it pounding violently against the darkness that traps her.

He was supposed to find me!

Her eyes roll back in her head and she whispers a final scream.

EIGHT

When Everly wakes up, she's drenched in sweat and breathing fast. Her pregnancy pillow, which cradles her and divides the bed between her and Brooke, is slicked with sweat too. Her heart is racing and the migraine that began at dinner is still pounding at the back of her brain. She sighs, trying to relax her muscles as they clench and strain. She tries to get comfortable in the bed, flipping her pillow to the cold side and sweeping her hair off her face.

Beside her, Brooke groans in her sleep as she tosses and turns. Her wife has always been a light sleeper and, for a moment, Everly is worried that her nightmare has woken them both. But eventually, Brooke is still and snoring softly.

Although she closes her eyes and tries to sleep, Everly feels too awake and warm to rest. She turns onto her back and stares up at the skylight window, the rain from the storm beating against the glass. Her eyes are just starting to get heavy when she sees the tiny cracks splitting the surface of the window, forming a spider web pattern that she's seen before in the nursery and on her glass and... She struggles to remember. She knows she's seen these same cracks elsewhere, but her mind is drawing a blank.

She frowns as a drop of water falls through the thin crack and onto the bed. She sits up and watches in disbelief as it soaks into the cotton, leaving a small amber mark on the white sheet. Another drop slowly makes its way through the crack in the glass, staining the bed in another spot. She looks up as the drops begin to fall more rapidly, steadily turning the white bed orange. One drop lands right on her lips, and it's the familiar and bitter taste of pennies.

Of rust.

That's when it clicks.

"The car," she whispers to herself.

He was supposed to find me.

"Oh my God, you're in the car!" she shouts.

Brooke's eyes shoot open and she sits up in the bed as Everly scrambles to get out.

"What's wrong? What's going on?"

Everly doesn't have time to explain. Instead, she stumbles down the stairs, grabs the spare house key on the table in the entranceway, and flies out the front door as her wife jogs after her.

"Eve, what are you doing?" Brooke calls, her words muffled by the rain.

Everly unlocks the garage, looking for the right tools as Brooke follows her inside. Although the two women have only been in the rain for a few seconds, their nightgowns are already soaked.

"Everly, stop!" Brooke shouts. "What the fuck are you doing?"

"He's in the *car*!" Everly gasps, horrified.

"*Who?*"

"Zachary!"

"What are you talking about?"

Everly scans the wall of tools, eyes passing over shovels and spades and an old rake.

"The crack in the glass," Everly says, spotting the tool she's been searching for. "I'd seen that pattern somewhere, but I couldn't remember where. It was driving me nuts, but then I remembered I'd seen it before on the passenger's window of the Beetle."

"Okay? So?"

Everly unhooks the hatchet from the wall and takes it out of its sheath.

"Patty said that Zachary went missing during a game of hide-and-seek," she says, nodding her head.

"Okay. And?"

"And I'm thinking that he found some way to crawl

into the car and couldn't get back out."

Everly turns to walk back out into the rain, but Brooke stops her with a hand on her arm.

"Eve, this is nuts," she says, exhausted. "Put the hatchet back and let's go back to sleep."

"He's in the car, Brooke, I'm sure he is. I can feel it in my bones."

"Can't it at least wait until morning?"

Everly looks out into the yard. In the distance, she's sure she can make out a small heart-shaped face staring back at her through the rain.

"No, it can't."

"So, what, you're going to cut down an entire elm with that thing?"

"If I have to."

Brooke rolls her eyes as Everly marches out of the garage and across the lawn, the mud and wet grass squishing between her bare toes as she approaches the car. The rain falls in curtains and she has to squint against the water that tries to get into her eyes. She stands at the back of the car, where the elm and the Beetle look like they converge, and she lifts the hatchet.

"Stop!" Brooke calls out to her.

Everly looks over her shoulder, and her eyes widen as she steps out of Brooke's way.

The other woman approaches with a chainsaw, a pair of work gloves and safety goggles standing out in harsh contrast to her oversized yellow nightgown.

"I *really* hope you have a secret savings account I don't know about."

"Why?"

"Because you'll need it to pay the massive ticket we're about to get and then to bail me out of jail when they arrest me. Now get back," she tells Everly, before starting the machine up and lowering it against the tree.

The chainsaw is loud and rips through the sounds of the rain and the thunder. Brooke cuts away the thick branches, avoiding making too much of a dent in the trunk as she works. The last thing either of them needs is an old tree crushing them or falling on top of someone's house. It takes her a while to strip the thick branches back, and more than once Brooke cusses loudly as the chainsaw accidentally strikes rust that's hidden in the elm. When she's as satisfied as she can be with her work, she brings the machine back to the garage as Everly stands over the exposed trunk of the Beetle.

The metal of the trunk is blue and less rusty than the rest of the car, but it's heavily warped and misshapen thanks to the accident and the elm. The trunk is caved in, almost flat, and the handle to open it is unrecognizable. When Brooke comes back, she's carrying a crowbar, a mallet, and a spade, the latter of which she hands to Everly.

"Don't strain yourself," she tells her wife, nodding to Everly's bulging stomach. "The last thing I want is to have to take you to the hospital tonight. Okay?"

Everly nods.

Brooke presses the tip of the crowbar against the base of the trunk, steadying it with one hand as she strikes the other end with the mallet. Slowly, she forces it under the metal lip and begins to work to pry it open. Once the trunk has lifted a bit more, she takes the spade and jams it into the crack too. It's slow work, and by the time they start seeing progress with the back hatch, Everly is shivering.

"You should go inside."

Everly shakes her head, pushing down on the handle of the tool. She doesn't tell Brooke it's because she can feel Zachary watching her in the rain, his eyes the only thing she can make out in the downpour.

"I need to see. I need to know for sure."

After that, the two of them work silently. The only noises punctuating the air between them are the sound of rain, the rumble of thunder, and the crash of lightning in the distance. She hopes they'll be done soon; the last thing she wants is lightning flashing overhead as she holds a metal shovel next to a rust pile under a tree. Eventually, the trunk begins to give, and with a final strain, the two women hear the loud click of the latch giving out.

Everly knows what she's going to see before she sees it, but that doesn't make the sight any easier.

The bones are how she imagined they might be from the dream. One arm is pinned to his side, the other is next to his face, dented metal and heavy tools pressing against him. From the look of it, he'd managed to crawl into the trunk using a hole under the car from where the engine must have fallen out during his father's accident. Unfortunately for the boy, his crawling must have knocked the car off its blocks, preventing his escape and knocking the heavy tools on top of his too-small body.

His skull and one hand are pressed against the leather of the back seats. He'd managed to claw a small hole in the leather and cotton stuffing, but with the way his head was turned, the only thing Everly suspected he could see was the cracked window on the passenger's side. Her chest hurts as she sees the way his legs are curled up against his body, his feet pressed against the corner of the trunk where she'd felt vibrations and banging, like he'd been kicking for help. Had it been a modern car, he may have been able to lower the back seat and crawl into the cabin of the vehicle.

Unfortunately for Zachary, it hadn't been, and he'd been crushed to death.

"Oh my God," Brooke breathes as she looks down at the small boy.

Everly doesn't hear her wife, her attention now focused on the small boy in his dirty jeans.

For the first time, his eyes are filled with relief, not fear. His face is illuminated by the glow of the dim street lamps, and he waves a hand to Everly with a wide grin before turning his back to her.

"My turn, Dillon. Ready or not, here I come!" he shouts into the darkness.

Everly watches him run down the driveway, giggling to himself as he chases after his brother, his body dissipating into the rain.

 NINE

"If you're going to go by the store, you might also want to grab more wipes," Everly reminds Brooke as she passes her wife the diaper bag. "He should have enough, but you never know with this little guy."

She leans over and kisses the top of Zachary's head, but he's too comfortable in his Babybjörn strapped to Brooke's chest to notice. Although Brooke had been against the name at first, thinking it was too morbid to give their son, Everly had eventually won out.

"Yeah, I'll pick up more on the way over."

"And you're *sure* you don't mind me staying home? I always feel bad skipping out on seeing your mom."

"You see her more than I do. I'm sure it's fine if you miss one dinner."

Brooke adjusts the bag on her shoulder before leaning in to give Everly a kiss.

"I love you," she whispers.

"I love you more," Everly says back.

She leans against the frame of the front door, watching as Brooke straps their son into his car seat before tossing the diaper bag into the trunk, getting into the car, and driving off.

As Everly watches her wife drive away, she can't help but think about how empty their front yard looks now. After the child's body had been discovered, the rusted Beetle had been removed from the premises. Although they'd tried to save what was left of the elm tree, it too had eventually been removed and replaced with a sapling. Although they'd had to pay out of pocket to cut down the elm and plant another one, Brooke had just been grateful they'd dodged a fine and incarceration.

Once the Toyota has faded from view, she closes the front door and breathes a sigh of relief knowing that, for the first time since moving into the house at 23 McCormick Road, she's well and truly alone.

A NOTE FROM
DARKLIT PRESS

All of us at DarkLit Press want to thank you for taking the time
to read this book. Words cannot describe how grateful we are
knowing that you spent your valuable time and hard-earned
money on our publication. We appreciate any and all feedback
from readers, good or bad. Reviews are extremely helpful for
indie authors and small businesses (like us). We hope you'll
take a moment to share your thoughts on Amazon, Goodreads
and/or BookBub.

You can also find us on all the major social platforms including
Facebook, Instagram, and Twitter. Our horror community
newsletter comes jam-packed with giveaways, free or deeply
discounted books, deals on apparel, writing opportunities, and
insights from genre enthusiasts.

ABOUT THE AUTHOR

Caitlin Marceau is a queer author and lecturer based in Montreal. She holds a Bachelor of Arts in Creative Writing, is an Active Member of the Horror Writers Association, and has spoken about genre literature at several Canadian conventions. She spends most of her time writing horror and experimental fiction, but has also been published for poetry as well as creative non-fiction. Her work includes *Palimpsest, Magnum Opus*, and her debut novella, *This Is Where We Talk Things Out*. Her second collection, *A Blackness Absolute*, and her debut novel, *It Wasn't Supposed To Go Like This*, are set for publication in 2023. For more, check out her website at CaitlinMarceau.ca or find her on social media.

CONTENT WARNINGS

GASTRIC

Fatphobia

Disordered Eating

Emetophobia

IN UTERO

Self-mutilation

Death of a child

DARKLIT
PRESS

Made in the USA
Columbia, SC
27 December 2022

74158040R00136